AN EYRE OF MYSTERY

A LITERATIA NOVEL

G. LEESON

GRACE ABRAHAM PUBLISHING

Grace Abraham Publishing
A Division of Washington Cooper, Inc.
13335 Holbrook St., Suite 10
Bristol, Virginia 24202

Publisher's note: This is a work of fiction. Names, characters, places, and incidents are a product of the author's imagination. Locales and public names are sometimes used for atmospheric purposes. Any resemblance to persons living or dead, or to businesses, companies, events, institutions, or locales is completely coincidental.

Book Cover Design 2022 by Cover Villain.

Ordering information:
Special discounts are available on quantity purchases by corporations, associations, and others. For details, contact the "Special Sales Department" at the above address.

An Eyre of Mystery/G. Leeson – First edition
ISBN: 978-1-7373009-3-9

AN EYRE OF MYSTERY

CHAPTER 1

Where am I? These buildings...the streets—nothing looks normal. Nothing looks modern. And the smell. Ugh. It nearly made me gag. I looked down and saw I was standing beside a pile of fresh horse dung. The horse swished its tail as it passed.

"—goa raight to t' divil then!"

"Huh?" At the sound of the brusque female voice, I raised my chin. "Are you talking to me?"

She was. Or, rather, she had been. Now the forbidding old woman dressed like she'd just stepped out of a Brontë novel shook her head, put her nose in the air, and strode on. What was that she'd said? Was it even English?

Realizing my own clothes felt a bit strange, I glanced down at the fancy, floor-length skirt I was wearing. It was a dark red satin with white and gray stripes. I imagined the bonnet tied at my throat matched it.

Am I in costume? Maybe I was in a play. No. There wouldn't be real horse dung in a play. Besides, I wasn't on a stage.

Either way, I needed to get my butt out of the middle of the road.

My mind raced as I hurried to the sidewalk. *What's the last thing I remember? I was in the library and saw that odd glowing letter* L *on the cover of* Jane Eyre. *I touched it and—*

"Now then. Come along."

It was Mr. Briggs. I knew him. I mean, I didn't *know* him and didn't know *how* I knew him, but…but I did. He was Mr. Briggs, the attorney from *Jane Eyre*. He led me down the macadamized street.

"Wh-what are we doing?" I asked.

"He's asked for you, and you indicated you wanted to see him." He frowned down at me. "Have you changed your mind?"

"No." I reached out and took Briggs' arm—I needed the support, but I also craved proof he was real. He was. As real as anything in this place. Had I fallen? Hit my head? Was this a dream? If so, it was the most vivid I'd ever experienced.

Briggs escorted me into a prison and spoke briefly with a jailer, who then led us to a cell. I was behind Briggs, so I couldn't see inside the cell at first.

The jailer pinched my shoulder.

I yelped in surprise and glared at him. "What was that for?"

"You don't belong here." His voice was a menacing hiss; and when he bared his teeth at me, a silverfish darted through them.

The tingling started at my scalp and worked its way through my spine. Still, I managed to lift my head slightly. I inherently knew I couldn't show this creature any hint of fear.

Briggs moved aside, and I turned away from the jailer and stepped closer to the bars.

"Edward," I whispered. Edward Rochester, the brooding hero of *Jane Eyre*.

"Jane. Darling, Jane." He reached for my hands through the bars.

I put my hands out, and he squeezed them.

Staring into my eyes, he said, "Wait. You aren't—" He addressed Mr. Briggs then. "May we have a bit of privacy?"

"Of course. I'll be in the other room with the jailer." Mr. Briggs patted my forearm before walking away.

"Who are you?" Edward asked quietly.

"I'm Gia."

"Did Cooper send you?"

Cooper—the man who'd hired me as archivist for the Smithmore Manor library this morning.

"Yes," I said. Maybe Cooper had sent me, and maybe he hadn't, but *yes* seemed to be the safest answer under the circumstances.

Edward blew out a breath of relief. It wasn't pleasant.

Didn't they have toothpaste in the 1840s? Gum? Mints? I'd have to look into that.

"What are you doing in prison?" I asked.

"I'm to be hanged in five days for the murder of my wife."

"Murder? No one killed Bertha. She committed suicide after setting the fire."

He shook his head. "There was no fire, and Bertha was murdered."

"You—?"

"No," he interrupted. "Not me. You need to find out who did kill her and work with Briggs to get me exonerated. I'm from your world; but if I die in this world, I'm dead in both." He paused. "Same goes for you."

I gulped. "That's good to know."

It wasn't, Reader. It wasn't good to know in the slightest.

"We have few allies here and many enemies."

"Oh, I've already made an enemy," I said. "The jailer pinched me! Then he told me I didn't belong here. And when I looked up at him, there was a silverfish in his mouth. Do you people not have toothpaste?"

"He is a silverfish. They destroy books. You're here to preserve the book—and, hopefully, my life."

"Okay, how do I—?"

"Time to go, Miss Eyre." Briggs had returned.

"Please," I said, "can't we have a few minutes more? I have so many questions."

"The jailer won't permit it. Perhaps we may return in a day or two."

"A day or two? We only have five!"

Edward pressed my hands before letting them go. "Cooper must have faith in you, so I do as well. Go and use the utmost caution."

I nodded. *What have I gotten myself into?*

BRIGGS HELPED me into a hansom cab and instructed the driver to take me to Thornfield Hall.

Thornfield Hall—the Rochester home. I tried to swallow the lump that had formed in my throat. *Wonder what awaits me there?*

"I have things to attend to in town, my dear, but I'll be around to check on you later this afternoon," he told me.

There weren't any silverfish in his mouth, as far as I could tell. I thanked him and was relieved for some time alone.

Taking a closer look at my outfit, I had to admit that the person who'd fashioned it had done an excellent job. It certainly felt authentic. The reticule hanging from my left wrist was gray with a floral bouquet embroidered on the front and tassels at the corners. I'd noticed the purse earlier but now took the opportunity to see what was inside—hopefully, a piece of hard candy for my uncomfortably dry mouth.

I untied the drawstring and pulled the fabric apart. Inside was a small fan, some coins, a lace-edged handkerchief, and a folded piece of tan paper. Snatching the paper out of the purse, I opened it and read:

Gia, if you're reading this, you've taken your first journey into Literatia. Congratulations! No, you aren't crazy; you aren't dreaming; you aren't comatose; you aren't dead; you aren't whatever else you might believe you are. You're actually in another world—a book world—and you must recalibrate that world before the silverfish entirely destroy the book. But no worries. I have the utmost faith in your abilities. Fond regards, Cooper Wellingham

Staring down at my employer's words, I said aloud, "This *has* to be a dream."

The words on the note immediately disappeared and were replaced with: *It isn't. I already told you that.*

"Wait. I can talk with you using this paper?"

Again, like some sort of weird voice-to-text device that worked in reverse or backward or upside down or something, the paper was erased, and new words appeared.

In a way. I told you when you accepted the job this morning that you were taking on a challenging role. You indicated you enjoyed challenges.

"Well, yeah, but not sci-fi, world-hopping challenges that include people with silverfish in their teeth. This is way too out of the box for me."

Had I believed you were not up to the task, I'd have never allowed you to embark upon this journey. If you aren't receptive, I need to pull you out and get someone inside who is willing to help Mr. Rochester immediately.

"I never said I wasn't willing to help Mr. Rochester." I huffed. "Of course, I am. I just—" I chewed on my lower lip for a second. "Get in here and help me already."

Unfortunately, I cannot. I'd be recognized immediately in Literatia, and the silverfish would work quickly to devour the book and everything in it. That includes Mr. Rochester and you in case you hadn't guessed.

"Mr. Rochester told me that if we die in the book, we die. Period. Am I getting hazardous duty pay for this gig? Because we never talked about my risk of dying. I figured my biggest threat would be a papercut."

Finish your task successfully, and you will be rewarded.

I wasn't making myself clear. I needed to reframe my question and stop being flippant. "What are the odds of my dying here?"

The words previously written faded out, but new words didn't come right away.

"Did you hear me?" I asked.

Low. Under all but the most extreme circumstances, I will be able to extricate you before you die.

"Oh." I slumped against my seat in relief. "And you can get Rochester out too, right?"

No. His life is in your hands.

"But he's your guy. He knew you sent me before *I* knew you sent me. You can't just leave him in there. In fact, why can't you take us both out of here now?"

I'm unable to remove Rochester. If I get you out, Rochester will die, and the literary classic Jane Eyre *will never have existed. That has farther-reaching ramifications in our world and in Literatia than you realize. I will ask you once again, are you up to this challenge?*

"I am."

Good.

"I'll keep this paper with me at all times so that I can communicate with you as necessary."

This is the only communication we can have until you return. If you were to be found with this paper, you'd be hanged as a witch.

"The last witch hanging in England took place in the late 1600s."

Trust me, they'll make an exception. Now, I'll leave you with a few words of clarification: Not everyone is who they seem or have the same personalities as those they originally embodied in the book. One of those characters killed Rochester's wife. Bring that person to justice, free Rochester, and you will be brought home. Godspeed.

Starting at one corner, the paper turned to ash. I realized Cooper was burning it on the other side. I brushed it onto the floor of the cab and watched it completely turn to dust.

This morning I'd started what I guessed would be a boring but nice job as an archivist at a gorgeous manor house in the hills of North Carolina. Now it wasn't even lunchtime, and I was responsible for a man's life, trying to avoid being killed myself, and tasked with keeping *Jane Eyre* safe for readers everywhere.

The cab came to a stop. I took out a coin and pulled

the drawstring to close my reticule when I heard the driver climbing down from his seat.

"I thought I heard you talking," he said, upon opening the door and helping me out. "Me wife was a praying woman too."

I smiled. "Too bad she isn't here. I could use all the help I can get."

CHAPTER 2

I straightened my shoulders, set my face, and strode into Thornfield Hall like I owned the place. The house was massive—way bigger than I thought it would be. I remembered Jane describing Mr. Rochester's abode as being one of considerable size, but she didn't tell me how small and frightened I'd feel once I'd entered it. And yet I kept up my charade of bravado.

Thornfield Hall was cavernous and drafty. The clang of the door shutting echoed in the great hall. I was glad it was summer and that I didn't have to worry about freezing to death. Even so, I shivered a little as I looked at the mirror over the mantel. My reflection blurred and changed. I stepped closer.

Who is that?

Looking behind me, I saw that I was still alone in the room.

It's me. But it isn't me. It's—

"Jane, I didn't hear you come in."

Mrs. Alice Fairfax, the housekeeper. She fit her description in the novel to a tee, down to her white widow's cap and black silk dress. It made sense that somehow the other characters would see me as Jane, but I didn't realize I wouldn't look like me...to me.

"That's all right, Mrs. Fairfax. I know you're busy."

"Quite so, but that is no excuse for not seeing to your nourishment. I appreciate how you fret over Mr. Rochester, but you are ever so pale and thin." She smiled then.

I gasped when a silverfish scrambled up over her gums.

"What is it, dear?"

"Um..." I put my fingers up to my temple. "I-I had a pain in my head. I must be overtired. I think I shall go up and have a lie down."

"Of course."

Go up and have a lie down? Is that the proper vernacular? I don't want to give myself away—especially to the silverfish— but they already know, don't they? The jailer had known. I have to believe Mrs. Fairfax knows as well. But maybe they don't know I know about them. Maybe they don't realize I can see the silverfish in their teeth.

I took the oak staircase up to my room. White, yellow, and pink roses—cut from the gardens outside—were in a vase on a table by my bed. I took off my bonnet—I'd been right that it matched the dress—and placed it and my reticule on the table. If I'd had my smartphone with me, I could've taken a photo of the bonnet, reticule, and roses and maybe submitted it to an antiques magazine. Too bad I *didn't* have my phone.

Reader, I needed the internet.

Taking silverfish and imminent death out of the equation, I was able to separate my situation from my surroundings and admit that my room was beautiful. The bed was a canopied four-poster made of ornate mahogany. There was a fireplace, a wardrobe, and a dressing table with two small drawers on each side and a mirror in the center. An open-backed chair was tucked beneath the dressing table.

I pulled out the chair and sat at the dressing table. An ornate brush, comb, and mirror sat on a mirrored tray. A blue porcelain jar contained hairpins, and—yes!—there was a tin of tooth powder.

Opening the tin, I smelled the tooth powder.

Bleh. Plus, what if old Silverfish Fairfax poisoned it? Could she be the Thornfield Hall murderer? If she'd killed Bertha Mason Rochester, why not rub out Jane as well?

Though my dressing table mirror was slightly cloudy, I leaned forward to peer at my reflection—or, rather, Jane Eyre's reflection. Her face was smaller than mine, and she had a sharp, pointed chin. Instead of my blonde hair, Jane's hair was—at first glance—a flat brown; but upon turning my head this way and that until it caught the sun streaming through the window, I could see some soft caramel highlights.

Downstairs, I hadn't recognized myself. And yet

Edward Rochester had known almost immediately that I wasn't Jane. How had he known? I'd have to ask him.

Putting thoughts of my appearance out of my head, I searched through the drawers to see what else I could find to work with. To be succinct, not much. Not only did I not have a phone or the internet, but I also didn't have a car or electricity to help me solve this mystery and clear Edward Rochester of murder. However, if memory and Jane's narrative served, I had an extensive library at my disposal.

I got up and headed for the stairs. In the hallway, I met Grace Poole, the woman who'd been tasked with the care of Bertha Rochester in the original novel. Most of her red hair was hidden under a widow's cap, and she wore a gray dress covered with a white apron. She grasped my arm, and I flinched.

"Sorry to startle you, pet, but did you see the master of the house today?" she asked.

Maybe I was mistaken. Maybe this wasn't Grace Poole after all.

"I did."

"And how did he look? Are they giving him enough to eat?"

Not knowing what she hoped I'd say, I shrugged.

She clucked her tongue. "Poor man. I know he didn't do what he's been accused of doing. I understand as well as anyone what a burden the missus was, what with all her maladies, but Mr. Rochester took care of her the best that he could. As did I." She shook her head. "I was little more than a child when I first went into service with the Mason family. I hadn't the slightest idea what I was getting into."

Taking Miss Poole by the shoulders, I said, "I want you to lift your head up and give me a smile."

The bewildered woman hesitantly did as I asked, spreading her thin lips slightly in an expression that hovered somewhere between a wince and a grimace.

"Now, you can do better than that." I gave her a bright, toothy grin of my own. "We must bear up and have hope, you and I."

She gave me a true smile then, and although she was missing a bicuspid, I didn't see a silverfish slithering around in there.

"Right you are, miss. We must pray for a miracle."

"Miss Poole, do you know who might've wanted the missus to be—gone? Who stood to gain from her death?"

"Mr. Rochester, of course, which is why he's in the prison at this moment." Her smile was replaced by an expression of regret. "Although, while I do feel he'd be relieved to escape the burden of having such an ill wife, I don't think for an instant that it was he who stabbed her as she slumbered." She took a handkerchief from the pocket of her apron and dabbed at her eyes. "I was devastated to find her that way."

"If not Mr. Rochester, then who? Who would want to harm her?" I asked.

"I don't know. But I must get back to work, dear. I have to help get everything ready for tonight's dinner party." She patted my shoulder and mustered up another smile. "Bear up!"

"Wait—a dinner party?"

"Oh, yes. Everyone is coming to be with Adele in her time of misfortune. And now I must carry on before Mrs. Fairfax has my head."

"Of course. Thank you." Cooper's note had said that not everyone's personality would be that of their character in the book. That certainly would explain Grace Poole's warm, caring persona. But I also needed to remember that historically the person who "found" the victim was often the one who committed the murder.

Waiting until Grace was down the stairs and out of the way, I decided to check out Bertha Rochester's room. Hopefully, there would be some clue there to help me narrow down my list of suspects.

I half expected to find the room locked, but without Mrs. Rochester in it, why should it be? I went inside and quietly closed the door behind me. This room was dark and oppressive. The heavy curtains over the one window were shut. There were no mirrors. No candelabras. No dressing table. Only a bed, a washstand, a wardrobe, and a small chest of drawers.

How sad. Bertha Rochester had been imprisoned here in this miserable little room simply because she was mentally ill. And this place hadn't helped matters in the slightest. Who wouldn't go mad—or madder—locked in here?

I crossed to the window and opened the curtains.

Dust motes floated on the air. I blinked against the sudden light in the room.

When my eyes adjusted, I scanned the room again. There were a brush and comb on the chest. No hairpins or lotions or knitting needles or books that I could see. I imagined Grace Poole brought in things as needed and took them away again before Bertha could use them to hurt herself or someone else.

I went through the drawers. They held linens and little else. Before I turned toward the wardrobe, I spotted something glistening in the corner. I bent and picked it up. It was a brass button. I slipped it into my pocket.

The wardrobe held nothing notable; and when I peeped under the bed and saw a chamber pot, I decided I was done in this room. I went to the library.

Adele, the girl for whom Jane had been hired as governess, was sitting at a table poring over a botany textbook.

"Hello, Adele," I said.

She didn't look up. "Hello."

"Your book must be really interesting."

"Quite."

So, no loquacious butterfly here—this Adele was all business.

Sitting across from her, I said, "I apologize for interrupting you, but I wanted to make sure you're all right."

She looked up, nodded, and returned to her book.

I wasn't having any of her attitude. As her governess, surely I had some authority over her. I reached out and took the book. I kept it open to the page Adele had been reading but placed the book on my lap and folded my arms over it.

She glared at me. "What is it you want?"

"I want to speak with you."

"About what?" she asked.

"About Mr. Rochester, for one thing. Are you concerned about him?"

"Not particularly. If he killed Bertha, then he deserves his punishment."

"I believe Mr. Rochester is innocent," I said. "Don't you?"

Lifting her thin shoulders, she said, "The judge said he is guilty. It was for him to say, not me."

"Still, you are entitled to your opinion. Did Mrs. Rochester have any enemies?"

"Everyone was her enemy, except for that simpering Miss Poole," Adele said. "The rest of the household hated her—including you."

"I didn't hate her. I didn't even know her."

"Perhaps not, but anyone with eyes can see you are in love with the master of Thornfield Hall. Were he not headed for the gallows, you could marry him now."

I handed back her book and stood to peruse the shelves. I much preferred the original version of Adele. This one was far too precocious for her—or my—own good.

I quickly became enamored of the books I found: a leather-bound set of the works of Shakespeare, *A View of*

Society and Manners in Italy by John Moore, a King James Version of the Holy Bible, *A Word of Remembrance and Caution to the Rich* by John Woolman, *Outlines of Lectures on Mental Diseases* by Sir Alexander Morison.

That last one stopped me in my tracks. Had Edward been trying to find a way to help Bertha? I sandwiched the book by Morison between the one by John Woolman and a book by Coleridge and carried them out of the library. Maybe I could find a quiet place in the courtyard where I wouldn't be disturbed.

The scents of lilies and primroses drew me to the garden where I sat on a stone bench. It was beautiful here, and the garden was well tended. Behind the boxwood hedges were beds of daisies, narcissus, dahlias, valerian, and foxglove.

Foxglove—digitalis.

My mind went back to Adele's book on botany. Miss Poole had said Bertha was stabbed to death. But what if she'd been given something to make her sleep more deeply first? I'd be wise not to trust anyone in this place.

CHAPTER 3

"Ah, here you are," Mr. Briggs said, when he found me in the garden.

I managed a slight smile. "I needed some air."

"Understandable." He sat beside me on the bench.

He wasn't as old as I'd imagined him to be when I'd read *Jane Eyre*. I now guessed him to be in his mid-to late thirties.

"Are you married, Mr. Briggs?" I asked.

Lowering his head as he chuckled, he answered, "No, Miss Eyre. My wife died in childbirth some years ago."

I wanted to ask about the child, but I'd already been too forward already. Instead, I told him about my chat with Miss Poole. "She told me how terrible it was when she found 'the missus' stabbed to death."

"Yes, it would have shaken anyone to his or her very core."

"Still, I can't understand the judge's logic in

condemning Edward," I said. "He and his wife didn't share a room, he didn't visit her often." I drew in a deep breath. "Tell me about the trial as if I wasn't even there. Maybe some clue will present itself if we go over everything step-by-step—some notion as to how we can save Edward from the gallows."

He squinted at me as he rubbed his chin, but he decided to humor me. "There wasn't much of a trial once the letter was produced."

"What letter?"

"Oh, my, you really *are* playing devil's advocate, aren't you? I'm, of course, speaking of the note Bertha left saying that if any harm befell her, inquiries of Edward Rochester should be made."

"And how was the judge convinced that Bertha truly wrote this letter? Anyone could have written it to cast suspicion onto Edward."

"Well, not *anyone*," he reminded me gently.

That's right. Few of the servants are literate.

"Perhaps Grace Poole persuaded Mrs. Rochester to write the letter," I said. "Someone who had Bertha's ear as Grace Poole certainly did could have convinced the woman that Edward might try to harm her." As I watched a butterfly take flight from one blossom to another, my mind was whirling. "Is it possible Mrs. Rochester was having an affair?"

"Whyever would you ask that?"

Once again, I'd incensed Mr. Briggs with my brazen questions. "In the book—"

Oh, crap. What have I done? In the book, it was implied that Bertha had a number of affairs prior to living at Thornfield Hall. But, of course, Mr. Briggs didn't realize he was a character in a classic novel.

"Book?" Mr. Briggs asked. "What book? Did Bertha keep a journal?"

A journal. That works.

"It's only gossip. I shouldn't be repeating it."

"Miss Eyre, if Bertha Mason Rochester kept a diary, she might have confessed to writing the letter about Edward in order to spite him. Or she might have spoken of someone else she believed to be a threat to her." He stood and began to pace. "A diary would also give us the opportunity to compare a sample of Bertha's known handwriting against that of the note."

"Really? Handwriting analysis is a thing now?"

Reader, I needed to stop saying everything that passed through my mind.

"I don't know how much credence such a comparison would be given, but it could shed some doubt on the validity of the note."

"True."

He sat back down. "Miss Eyre, if such a book exists, you must find it and take possession of it as soon as possible. Say nothing to anyone and bring it to me. It might produce the evidence we need to exonerate Edward."

"And what course of action do we have if there is no diary?" I asked.

"I did all I knew to do at trial and was unable to successfully defend my client. You must recover that diary, if in fact there is one."

I nodded. As far as I knew, there was no diary. It was apparent from my inspection of Bertha's room that she had only the barest of necessities at her disposal. Still, I'd check with Grace Poole.

FOLLOWING my visit with Mr. Briggs in the garden, I went in search of Grace Poole. That was useless—the entire household was still bustling around preparing for the dinner party and the onslaught of houseguests.

I retrieved my bonnet and reticule from my room before slipping outside to the stables. Watching my step, I walked gingerly into the barn to find one of the grooms mucking out a stall.

"Hello." I smiled. "Could you please hitch up a carriage and drive me into town?"

He looked undecided for a moment, but then he capitulated. "Be ready in a jiffy."

"Thank you." I lifted my skirts and strode outside to wait. The thought struck me that there might be a new note in the purse. I stopped, opened the reticule, and looked inside. No such luck. I wondered if Cooper would receive it if I put a note to him in there. I might try it later. But I had that "hanged as a witch" thing to consider. Trying to contact "the other side" should probably be a last resort.

I hadn't been able to fully appreciate the town when I was there earlier. How could one value something they expected to wake up from any second? Now I saw how lovely and quaint a place it was, I was eager to see what I could find in the shops.

As the groom helped me out of the carriage, he asked, "Are you not taking a basket, Miss Eyre?"

"A basket?" *I'm supposed to have a basket?* "Yes! I am!" I forced a laugh. "I'm so flustered I nearly forgot it. Thank you for reminding me."

He hopped into the carriage and handed me a lidded wicker basket. I hung it on my arm, thanked him again, and told him I'd be back in half an hour.

The chemist's shop was an enchanting place with a myriad of glass bottles and porcelain jars. Red and white canisters advertised things I'd never heard of, so I was delighted when a label with the words *Cocoa Nut Oil* caught my eye.

I picked up a small bottle of something called *Chlorodyne*, which was *admitted by the Profession to be the most wonderful and valuable remedy ever discovered.* It said so right there on the label. It apparently cured everything from consumption to cholera, asthma to ague, diarrhea to dysentery.

"May I help you, miss?"

Glancing up from the bottle of wonder drug, I saw a

balding man wearing a stained white apron and round gold glasses peering at me.

"What is in this?" I asked.

He wagged an index finger at me. "I can't give away Dr. Browne's secret formula, but I will tell you it contains chloroform, cannabis, and laudanum. He recommends taking no more than thirty drops at a time, but I believe fifteen drops for a woman of your stature would be plenty. Even fewer, if you're buying for a child."

"A child?"

Reader, I was mortified that he wanted me to take the stuff, much less a child!

The chemist chuckled. "I take it you have no children then?"

"Not yet."

"Try not to put it off for too long. What will you be needing in addition to the Chlorodyne today?" he asked.

"Actually, I don't need the Chlorodyne. I'm looking for tooth powder."

"Right this way. Although, if you have a toothache, Chlorodyne will help." He came out from behind the counter and led me past the jar of leeches and the bottles of paregoric to the tins of tooth powder.

"That stuff must be good for whatever ails you," I said.

"Indeed."

I imagined you'd pass out until you got over whatever was wrong with you, or you'd simply die. I was less enchanted and more terrified of the chemist's shop now. One thing was certain—no one needed to be a botanist to procure a substance to sedate someone in Victorian England.

AFTER VISITING the chemist and finding toothpowder that probably wouldn't kill me and buying brushes and tins of toothpowder for both Edward and me, I went to the stationers and bought paper, ink, and a steel pen. On down the street, I wandered into the confectioners and bought vanilla and peppermint stick candy —hoping and praying there was no plaster of Paris in it.

How did anyone survive these good ol' days?

Almost out of money, I strolled toward the prison.

"Newspaper, miss?"

I turned to see a grubby-looking boy right out of central casting for *Oliver Twist* holding a newspaper out toward me.

"Sure." With a smile, I gave him my last coin. His wide eyes and slack jaw assured me I'd overpaid. That was fine with me. I was almost certain he needed the money more than I did.

After folding up the newspaper and tucking it into my basket, I went on to the prison.

"What're ye doin' back 'ere already?" the jailer asked me.

"I need to see Mr. Rochester for only a moment," I said. "I assure you I won't be long."

"Don't you worry. I'll see to that." He jerked his head in the direction of the cells.

Edward was sitting on his cot looking down at the floor. He glanced up at the sound of my approaching footsteps and smiled as he stood.

"What are you doing here?"

Reader, I was not particularly delighted that his words echoed those of the jailer.

"Here." I opened the basket and handed him his toothbrush, tooth powder, and candy sticks.

"Are you trying to tell me something?" he asked.

"Yes, I am."

He laughed. "Here I am concerned I'm about to hang, and you're worried about my dental hygiene."

"If you die, I want you to go with fresh breath."

"Does that mean you're going to kiss me goodbye?"

My eyes dropped to his full lips, and I realized I was not averse to kissing this man. "I hope it doesn't come to that. Do you know whether or not Bertha kept a journal?"

"No idea."

"Was she having an affair?" I asked.

He shrugged. "Anything is possible."

I took the button from my pocket. "I found this in her room. Is it yours?"

"No, but that is a gentleman's button—from a jacket or a waistcoat."

The jailer's chair scraped across the floor.

"I'd better go," I said. "But I'll do everything I can to get you out of this."

"I know." He broke off a piece of one of the vanilla candy sticks and popped it into his mouth. "Thanks for this."

"You're welcome."

The jailer was coming for me, but I headed him off. I didn't want him to see Edward's contraband before he could get it hidden.

"Thank you for your kindness," I told him.

He grinned a slimy, silverfishy smirk. "I can be kinder than this if given the chance."

Ignoring his gibe, I hurried from the prison.

The groom ushered me into the carriage. "Find everything you needed, miss?"

"I did. Thank you."

He closed the door and went to the driver's seat.

I reached into my basket and took out the newspaper. Could there possibly be anything helpful in it?

And there it was.

Eugene Francois Vidocq in Towne to Meet with Publisher

I banged on the side of the carriage. "Sir, stop! Please!"

The carriage came to a halt, and I heard the driver scrambling down.

He flung open the door. "Miss? What is it?"

"I need to deliver a note to the inn."

"Very well," he said. "I'll take you there."

As the carriage clattered along the uneven street

toward the inn, I pondered my rudimentary French. Naturally, the famed criminalist could speak English, but I wanted to cajole him into a meeting. Anything I might do to flatter him couldn't hurt—unless I misremembered an important word. Fate had put the first known private detective at my disposal, and I didn't want to blow it.

CHAPTER 4

Reader, I waited for a response.

And, fortunately, I didn't have to linger long. While I'd seen artists' renderings of the famous criminal turned detective, I really had no idea what to expect. The curly-haired septuagenarian wore gray pants, a navy waistcoat, and a white cravat. He walked with a cane but with such a jaunty step that I wondered if it was an affectation.

"*Bonjour*, my lovely," he said, taking my hand and raising it to his lips. "You wish a discourse with Vidocq?"

"I do."

He arched a bushy brow, and his eyes twinkled. "From your note, I surmise you wish to discuss a private matter. Shall we talk in my room?"

Tightening my lips into a firm line, I said, "My carriage is outside. Maybe we could take a drive around the square."

Vidocq threw back his head and laughed. "Ah, I see my reputation has preceded me."

"Yes, and I'd like to keep mine intact."

"I'll go get my coat and be right back," he said.

True to his word, he quickly returned. We went out to the carriage, and I instructed the driver to take us once around the square.

Vidocq climbed into the carriage and reached out a hand to help me up.

"The cane," I said. "Do you really need it?"

"One should never be without a cane." He winked. "Especially when one has as many enemies as Vidocq has."

I laughed.

"It's good to see you smiling. You have much on your mind." He sandwiched my hands between his. "Tell me all of it."

With no intention of telling him *all of it*, I said, "My name is Jane Eyre. My employer, Edward Rochester, is in prison for the murder of his wife. I need to prove his innocence."

"One, I perceive the man is more to you than your employer."

I inclined my head, choosing to neither confirm nor deny that statement. Yes, Edward was more to Jane than her employer. As to what Edward and I were to each other, I had no idea.

"Two, you are not Jane Eyre."

My jaw dropped.

Vidocq chuckled. "Did you not seek out Vidocq because he is the greatest of detectives?"

"What makes you think I'm not Jane Eyre?" I asked, realizing I'd forgotten to ask Edward how he'd known Cooper had sent me.

"I think you are not because you are not," he said simply. "It's obvious to me that you aren't from here. The eyes are the windows of the soul, *ma petite*, and yours—beautiful though they are—look upon everything here with both wonder and suspicion. Be honest with me, and I will help you. Continue in your deceit, and you may have your driver drop me off here."

"Okay. My real name is Gia, but everyone thinks I'm Jane Eyre. To them, I look like her. Heck, to *me*, I look like her. I caught a glimpse of myself in the mirror and nearly fainted."

He nodded. "I'm a master of disguise myself."

"Edward is innocent—I know he is—but to prove it and save his life, I must find out who actually killed Bertha Mason Rochester. I came to you because I've read your mem—um…I mean, I heard of your expertise and knew that if anyone can help me, it's you."

"I'm happy to offer my assistance."

"I…um…" I cleared my throat. "I don't have money."

With a cheeky grin, he said, "I'm sure we can work something out."

"Mr. Rochester will certainly pay your fee. I hope you were not thinking of trying to give me a lesson in a hayloft," I said, reminding him of the story in his memoirs where he told of being brutally beaten by four men when he was caught "about to give a lesson in a hayloft to a female scholar about sixteen years of age."

"*Pas du tout!* Not at all!" He laughed. "You *have* heard much about Vidocq."

"The hayloft incident—was it worth it, by the way?" I asked.

"It might have been had I been able to finish my lesson."

I laughed with him. "You're incorrigible."

"Ah, *oui*. You might have made me corrigible had you come into my life twenty years ago, eh, Gia?"

Eyes wide, I said, "You must call me *Jane*."

"I prefer *Gia*, but I'll do as I must. The next time you see me, I'll be in disguise as well. You must call me Father Francis."

"You'll be in disguise?"

"But of course! I'll be coming to dine with you," he said, "at Thornfield Hall."

"You know about Thornfield Hall?"

He rolled his eyes. "And you're trying to fool people into thinking you're the governess of that renowned place? Everyone knows about Edward Rochester, of Thornfield Hall, accused of killing his wife."

"Of course, they do." I slumped back against my seat.

"Have no fear, *ma petite*. I will come to you as a priest who has heard about the misfortune that has befallen Thornfield Hall, come to pray with its inhabitants." He winked.

"There's to be a dinner party tonight," I said.

"Excellent! I adore dinner parties."

The driver stopped. We were back at the inn.

Before the driver opened the carriage door, Vidocq tapped his index finger to his cheek.

"You are brazen, aren't you?" I whispered. Still, I kissed his cheek.

"Brazenness pays off, as you will soon see."

The driver opened the door.

Vidocq alighted and pressed a coin into the man's hand. "Thank you, *monsieur*. Please return after seeing Miss Eyre home and pick up my friend Father Francis, who is to dine at Thornfield Hall this evening."

"Yes, sir."

Turning to me, Vidocq said, "I hope to meet you again, Miss Eyre. It has been a pleasure conversing with you."

"Likewise."

The driver shut the door and left me to wonder how I was going to explain inviting a priest to Thornfield Hall when I hadn't the least authority to do so. If I'd had a seatbelt, I'd have buckled it. To paraphrase Bette Davis in *All About Eve*, it was going to be a bumpy night.

As soon as I returned to Thornfield Hall, I saw Grace Poole in the foyer.

"Grace, hi—hello!" I smiled. "I ran into a priest in

town—old friend of the Eyre family—and he'd heard about the family's...um...misfortune. He plans to come to dinner." I threw out that last part really quickly, hoping it would sail past her like a maple leaf on a stout breeze.

"He's coming to dinner?" She placed her hand on her ample chest. "I don't know that Mrs. Fairfax will be happy about that."

So much for sailing.

"Happy about what?" Mrs. Fairfax came into the hallway.

"We're having another dinner guest." Miss Poole spoke unabashedly, but she slid halfway behind me as she did so.

"Who?" Mrs. Fairfax demanded.

"Father Francis." I too spoke with a boldness I didn't quite feel. "He's been a great friend to the Eyres, as well as to many other people, and he's joining us this evening."

"Very well." The old woman sighed and then turned her glare on Grace. "See that another room is made ready."

I walked away with Grace. Lowering my voice to a whisper, I said, "That didn't go as badly as I'd feared."

"Nor I." She grinned. "You've got mettle—I'll grant you that."

We climbed the stairs, and I spoke again before Grace could go in the opposite direction. "Did Mrs. Rochester keep a diary?"

She snorted. "Heavens, no. And what would she have written about if she had?"

"I'm simply curious as to how the poor woman spent her days." I shrugged. "She must have been terribly lonely. I mean, of course, she had you, but I'm guessing you often had other things to do than tend to Mrs. Rochester."

"She lived a sad existence indeed, Miss Eyre. I spent as much time as I could with her." Grace looked down at the floor. "I don't mind telling you it wasn't always easy to be with the woman. She was ever so difficult. But she had other visitors too."

"Other visitors?" Yes! This could be just the information I needed. "Who?"

"Well, Mr. Rochester, for one."

"And there were others?" I tried not to let my desperation seep into my voice.

"Oh, sure—"

"Miss Poole!"

At the sound of Mrs. Fairfax's sharp voice, both Grace and I nearly jumped out of our skin.

"Is someone working on the room for Miss Eyre's unexpected guest?" she asked.

"I'm on my way to do that." Grace gave me a slight nod and hurried away.

"As for you," Mrs. Fairfax said, her voice now low and menacing, "I'm watching you."

CHAPTER 5

I went into my room, locked the door behind me, and lay down on the bed. It wasn't as soft as my bed at home and although the sheets didn't smell as nice, the scent wasn't terrible. I hoped I'd get back to my own bed in my own room in my own apartment before long.

After getting my bachelor's degree in library and information science, I had to come home from college to take care of my mother. She'd been pretty much home-bound for months, at which time, I worked at a book-store while earning my master's degree online. With my job, education, and caring for my mother, I'd had no time for a social life. When she'd died, I'd been left alone—every bit the orphan Jane Eyre had been. No siblings. I'd never known my dad. No boyfriend. And I'd been too busy for my friends.

No one would miss me if I died in this book world.

But I couldn't think like that. I was here. Before I

could leave, an injustice had to be righted. It was like a quest. I needed to draw on my knowledge of Victorian-era sleuths to determine how to solve Bertha's murder. I'd need to rely on cleverness, observation, talking, and snooping. I could handle that.

Remembering that early detectives regularly used disguises, I figured that was out of the question for me; but then, that's what I had Vidocq—or Father Francis—for.

When I found myself getting sleepy, I shook myself awake. I didn't have time to sleep—at least, not yet. I got up and went downstairs to the kitchen.

"Anyone need any help?" I asked, as the workers bustled around me.

The women either avoided my eyes or narrowed theirs at me with suspicion.

"Okay, well, let me know!" I took an apple, smiled, and left.

After polishing the apple within the folds of my skirt, I took a bite. It was crisp and sweet. I wandered into the library. Adele was sitting by the window doing embroidery.

Before I could ask her what she was making, Adele demanded, "Where have you been all day? Are we not having lessons anymore?"

"We are, but not until Mr. Rochester's…um…situation is resolved. I thought it would be respectful to wait."

"Until he's dead, you mean," she said.

"That's not at all what I mean. I'm praying justice will

be done and that Bertha's real killer will be found." I stared at the top of her bent head. "Don't you?"

She shrugged. "It doesn't matter all that much to me. My situation remains the same no matter what happens. I'll live here with my expenses overseen by Mr. Briggs until I marry."

I sat down across from her. "And that scares you?"

Looking up at last, she smirked. "Not really. Whether I like it or not, that's how things are."

"But you must be concerned—for Mr. Rochester, for whether or not you'll have a choice in who you marry, for—"

"You have more to be worried about than I do." She resumed her needlework. "I'm all you have at Thornfield Hall now. When I no longer need you, you'll have to seek employment elsewhere."

I blew out a breath, frustrated at her lack of empathy for Mr. Rochester—or for anyone, for that matter. "Who will be at the dinner party this evening?"

"The Rivers family is coming. I suppose you *could* go back to them when I no longer need you." She scowled at me. "But don't you remember that? Has Mr. Rochester's being arrested caused you to start going mad like Bertha?"

"Of course, I remembered that the Rivers are coming. I simply wondered who else will be here."

"Mr. Briggs—he's here already, Miss Ingram, and Uncle Dickie."

I guessed "Uncle Dickie" was Bertha's brother, Richard Mason.

"And I heard Mrs. Fairfax complaining about someone else who's coming," Adele continued. "Someone *you* invited. Who is he? Mr. Rochester's replacement?"

"His name is Father Francis."

She scrunched up her nose. "How dull. Oh, well, I can always count on Uncle Dickie to keep the party lively."

Although I didn't say so, I doubted Uncle Dickie's liveliness could hold a candle to that of Vidocq.

"I'll leave you to your embroidery."

Adele didn't respond, and I got up and went in search of Mr. Briggs. I found him in Mr. Rochester's study smoking a pipe and writing at the desk.

"I'd like to speak with you, but I'll come back if this is a bad time," I said from the doorway.

Mr. Briggs waved me in. "I'm merely working on a missive to request the judge to grant Edward a stay of execution."

"That's wonderful!" I hurried into the room and sat across the desk from Mr. Briggs, excited to hear his argument. "May I hear what you have so far?"

"I'd prefer to finish it first," he said.

"Of course."

"Besides, the judge isn't likely to grant my petition." He put the pen aside. "Now, what did you want to speak with me about?"

"Richard Mason," I said. "Will he receive any money

or other inheritance if and when both his sister and her husband are dead?"

My answer was a shrewd squint.

I elaborated. "Does Richard Mason stand to gain if Edward hangs for Bertha's death?"

"Yes, as a matter of fact, he does. Besides Adele, Mr. Mason is the person who would profit most upon Edward's death. But I don't think Richard Mason would have murdered his sister. And even if he had, how could he have known Edward would get blamed for the crime?"

"That's easy," I said. "He could've written the note that was supposedly from Bertha saying that Edward intended to harm her."

"You might be right." He took a puff from his pipe. "I shall have another talk with Mr. Mason."

"Let me do it. He won't be as suspicious of me."

"Very well."

"Wait—you said *another* talk. You've questioned him before?"

"Indeed."

"Because you had suspicions about him?" I asked.

"No, it was a matter of preparing for trial. If you'll recall, Mr. Mason was a character witness for Edward."

"Right. I simply thought—" I trailed off, not knowing what to say.

He pushed back his chair, came around to the front of the desk, and took both my hands. "We're all hoping for a miracle, my dear, but I don't believe Richard Mason murdered his sister."

"But we *know* Edward didn't," I said.

He squeezed my hands and said nothing.

"Mr. Briggs, you *do* believe Edward is innocent, don't you?"

"Of course. Of course, dear."

I wasn't convinced.

***

MY THOUGHTS WERE all over the place as I left the study and wandered down the hallway toward the stairs. I had less than five days to discover Bertha Mason Rochester's killer and prove Edward's innocence. But with Mr. Briggs not even convinced that Edward hadn't killed his wife, how could I pull off this coup?

Maybe when presented with evidence condemning the real murderer, Mr. Briggs would lead the charge and demand Edward's freedom.

Or maybe I could figure out a way to break Edward out of jail. Could we escape that way? Could Cooper then pull the two of us out of Literatia? Tomorrow I'd go to the jail and ask Edward. And if he didn't have the answer, perhaps he could tell me how to communicate with Cooper.

I felt better about my plan. Grandmother had always told me never to put all my eggs in one basket. Well, now

I had two baskets: find the real killer and have him or her convicted and Edward released; or break Edward out of jail and escape. That way, Edward wouldn't die. The book would continue—it would simply be different. Right?

In that vein, I supposed I *did* have one other option. Since Cooper had said he could take *me* out of Literatia at any time, I could confess to murdering Bertha myself. Then the judge would have to let Edward go. Even if he thought my confession was a ruse, it would have to be investigated. If nothing else, that would buy us more time.

The tiny hairs on the back of my neck tingled. I glanced over my shoulder and thought I saw someone ducking into an alcove. It was likely my imagination. Paranoia in overdrive.

Then I heard a door close. Okay, someone had been there, but not someone stalking me.

Shaking off the feeling, I walked up the stairs. I'd just reached the top, taken my hand off the railing, and turned toward my room when I was yanked backward down the stairs.

CHAPTER 6

I heard feet hurrying toward me from every direction. Grace was the first person I saw—her face was red and pinched as she patted my cheek.

Had I lost consciousness? I didn't think so, but—

"You young women need to stop scurrying up and down those stairs like so many rats." Mrs. Fairfax glared down at me. "I knew one of you would trip over the hem of your dress and fall one day. It's a wonder you didn't break your neck."

I got the feeling she wished I had.

Mr. Briggs stepped around Grace to take my hand. "Do you think you can stand? Is anything broken?"

"I don't think so." I tried to evaluate the pain radiating throughout my body. Most of it was in my head—literally, not figuratively.

"I'll carry you upstairs then."

As Mr. Briggs started to gather me into his arms, I

said, "I'm sorry—I mean, I don't think anything is broken. I do believe I can stand."

He helped me to my feet and allowed me a moment to get my bearings. I looked around to see who else had come to see about me.

"Shall I fetch the doctor?" Grace asked.

"No, thank you." I managed a slight smile. "I'm sure I'll be fine."

"Laudanum, then?" Mr. Briggs asked.

"N-not…not even that." I noticed Adele was smirking, and I widened my smile. "You didn't cause me to fall to get out of schoolwork, did you?"

"You know I didn't. In fact, you're the one who has put our lessons on hold." She looked up the stairs and then back at me. "I suppose I'd better be more watchful myself since the women of Thornfield Hall seem determined to fall prey to one misfortune after another."

"The women only?" I asked, dropping the pretense of a smile. "It seems to me Mr. Rochester is dealing with a great deal of misfortune of his own."

"Perhaps of his own making," Adele said.

"Besides," Mrs. Fairfax added, challenging me with her stare, "he isn't dead. Yet."

Mr. Briggs insisted on helping me up to my room, and Grace fussed over me once I was there. She fluffed my pillow and removed my shoes.

"Just lie here and rest for a while," she said. "You'll feel better by dinner."

"Please let me know when Father Francis gets here."

"I will."

I was relieved when Grace pulled the door shut and left me alone. My head throbbed, and I'd have loved to take a short nap, but I was afraid to let down my guard. I used an acupressure technique I'd picked up somewhere to try to ease the pain as I assessed my predicament.

There was no way I'd tripped on my hem, as Mrs. Fairfax had suggested. Had that been the case, I'd have fallen forward. No, someone had definitely pulled me backward, and it was more than likely one of the people who'd come to help me. Tonight, before going to sleep, I'd push that dresser in front of the door.

But how had someone slipped up behind me without my being aware? The stairs weren't terribly wide, but I still should have seen or heard someone approach. I'd have to investigate that mystery when I was feeling better.

On edge, I started when there was a knock at my door. "Grace?"

"No, it's St. John. May I come in?"

"Okay." I was still struggling to sit up when St. John—pronounced *Sinjin*—rushed into the room.

"Easy." He sat on the edge of the bed and took my face in his hands. "My darling Jane, are you all right? We've just arrived, and Miss Poole told us you'd taken a tumble."

"I'm fine."

He let go of my face and pulled me into a hug. This wasn't the cold St. John I was familiar with from the original novel, the man who'd asked Jane to marry him because she'd be a good wife for a missionary in India. He leaned back out of the hug and started to kiss me.

Nope, this is for sure not cold St. John! What is the nature of his relationship with Jane in this new iteration of the book?

Turning my face away, I said, "We don't want to set the entire household to gossiping. We should go downstairs."

He smiled, and I was immeasurably relieved that there were no silverfish in his teeth. "I adore that you are the epitome of propriety. I'm eager to make you my wife —the sooner, the better."

After giving me a chaste kiss on the cheek, he helped me out of bed where I put my shoes back on before we went downstairs. I wondered briefly if he'd looked as I'd slipped on the delicate boots. If so, he got quite a shot of ankle. Maybe now he'd believe me brazen and decide not to marry me.

I really need to get out of this place. It's starting to drive me insane.

St. John's sisters, Diana and Mary got up from the sofa and met us in the middle of the room.

Diana brushed a stray hair back off my forehead. "Are you well? We were told of your fall. I can help you get your hair back in order."

"Would you please?" I hadn't realized my hair wasn't in order. In fact, I hadn't given it a thought.

"Of course, dear. And we can do it right here. No need to climb those nasty stairs again."

That was a relief. Soreness had settled into my limbs, and I wasn't looking forward to traipsing upstairs to get my hair done.

"Mary, do you have a comb in your reticule?" Diana asked.

"No."

"You do," her sister insisted. "I saw you use it in the carriage."

"Very well," Mary said. "But you'll clean it afterward."

Gee whiz, this new Mary is a little ray of sunshine. She and Adele should get along great.

Mary begrudgingly turned over her comb to Diana, and Diana instructed me to sit on a chair by the window. Within about fifteen minutes and without making my head hurt much worse than it was already, Diana had me presentable again—at least, by her standards.

Not long after I'd had my hair done, Vidocq arrived in his Father Francis disguise. When he was shown into the living room, I got up out of my chair and all but sprinted over to kiss him on both cheeks.

Eyes dancing, he said, "Good evening, *ma petite*. I'm delighted to be here with you."

"And I'm so glad you're here," I said.

St. John came to stand beside me. "Who have we here?"

"This is Father Francis."

"How did the two of you become acquainted?" St. John asked.

Before I could answer, Vidocq walked further into the

room, sat on the chair I'd so recently abandoned, and began his elaborate tale.

"I was a friend of Jane's parents," he said. "I used to bounce the *bébé* Jane on my knee. Oh, she was so happy and so adored her Father Francis."

He could've stopped there, but *mais non!* He had a trowel and was laying it on thick.

"After little Jane lost her parents to typhus, we lost touch for such a long time. I didn't find her again until I officiated the wedding of Maria Temple of Lockwood School." He closed his eyes as if he were fighting back tears. "For some reason—a nudge from my beloved Creator, I daresay—I was prompted to tell Miss Temple about my dear friends, the Eyres, and their precious daughter. She reunited me with Jane the very next day."

He opened his eyes, damp with tears, and crossed the room to where I stood. Putting his hands on my shoulders, he said, "How it pained me to leave Jane in that dreadful school." He turned so that he could gauge the expressions of his captivated audience. "But, alas, I had no choice. Only today did I find my sweet Jane again. The sight of her brought such joy to this old man's heart." He lowered his head. "Yet I'm much troubled by the hardships that have befallen Thornfield Hall."

"Thank you, Father Francis," I said. "May I get you a drink?"

"I wouldn't turn down a brandy."

I poured him a glass and then suggested we take a stroll through the garden before dinner.

"I'll go with you," St. John said.

"Stay with us," Diana told him. "Let Jane and her friend reminisce."

"Oh." He gave a slight chuckle. "Forgive me for not wanting to allow my future bride out of my sight."

"Go on, you two," Diana said.

I handed Vidocq his brandy, and we made our escape.

"Quite the leech, isn't he?" he asked, once we were outside.

"Yes. I wasn't anticipating him to be this way."

"You were thinking he might be in India already?"

"I did. At the least, I didn't think I'd see him here at Thornfield Hall." I frowned up at him. "How do you know so much about me—I mean, Jane?"

"It was a fine story, I wove, *non*?"

"You didn't answer my question."

Grinning, he said, "It wasn't difficult. I'm a brilliant detective—is that not why you asked me to come? Now, we haven't long, so we must concentrate on the murder of Bertha Rochester. Have you made any discoveries?"

"I found a man's button in Mrs. Rochester's chambers. It isn't Edward's, so it's possible she was having an affair."

"That's a strong possibility. I heard she was quite beautiful—also mad, but such a combination can be exciting!" He waggled his bushy eyebrows.

I shook my head. Vidocq, alias Father Francis, might prove to be more of a handful than I'd expected. But he was right—he was a terrific detective.

"I saw Adele studying a book on botany," I said, "and there are some potentially dangerous plants here in the garden."

He nodded. "I see that. But Mrs. Rochester was stabbed, *non?*"

"She was, but maybe her killer gave her some sort of sedative so she'd be in a deep sleep when she was attacked."

"Astute. Anything else?"

"Only this—I fell down the stairs earlier, and I'm positive someone here caused my accident."

"That means you must be extremely careful, *ma petite,* but also that you are making the progress."

CHAPTER 7

Vidocq and I went back into the house to find that Richard "Uncle Dickie" Mason and Blanche Ingram had arrived. Blanche was every bit as pretty and ostentatious as Jane had described her in the novel, but Adele didn't seem to be taken with her. No surprise, since Adele wasn't the animated, vivacious kid I'd expected to meet. But she did seem to adore Richard, who'd been a minor character in the original novel. When Vidocq and I walked into the parlor, Adele was clutching Richard's right arm and leaning her head against it.

"Good evening," I said. "I'd like you both to meet my friend, Father Francis."

Richard was either not inclined or not able to free his arm to shake hands with Vidocq, so he gave him a brief nod of acknowledgment. Vidocq responded in kind, his attention much more occupied with the lovely Blanche. I did hope he'd remember he was pretending to be a man of the cloth. Then again, even a man of the cloth might be tempted to check out that cleavage.

"I'm so glad you're here." Blanche sashayed over to take the clergyman's hand. "It's a relief to know that poor Edward won't go to his grave with unconfessed sins in his heart."

"He can go to hell for all I care," Richard said.

Blanche released Father Francis's hand as if it had burned her and rushed over to Richard's left side. "Oh, my poor Richard, I didn't mean to be insensitive. I know how you grieve for your sister."

"B-but you were a character witness at Edward's trial," I said to Richard, looking from him to Mr. Briggs.

"I shouldn't like to discuss that at dinner," Richard said. "Suffice it to say that I spoke the truth about the Edward I knew and was confident a just verdict would be handed down."

"I, for one, wouldn't want any man to die with a burdened soul," St. John said. "My sisters and I are here to comfort Jane and Adele while they await Mr. Rochester's end because Adele is of the utmost importance to Jane. She wants to make certain Adele will be well cared for when we depart for India."

I shot Vidocq an expression of helplessness which he read expertly.

"Mr. Rivers, tell me how you and Jane met," he said, diverting St. John from his talk of whisking me away to India.

With a slight smile, St. John got up and came to take

my hand. He spoke to the room at large, but he gazed at me. "I found Jane near my home one evening. She was cold and half-starved. The desolate girl had been walking for days, having fled this place after some sort of argument." His eyes flicked toward Adele.

In the novel, Jane had fled Thornfield Hall after learning Rochester had a wife he kept in the attic but was intending to go through with a wedding to Jane anyway. But apparently that wasn't the reason Jane had fled in *this* story. Jane had come back to work here rather than becoming a teacher in the village girls' school. This new development brought up all sorts of questions.

Had Jane known about Bertha all along? Had she still fallen in love with Edward? What had driven her away then? More importantly, what had brought her back? I realized I didn't know this Jane Eyre—the character, as well as the story. Was it possible *Jane* had killed Bertha Mason? No. If she had, she'd never let Edward take the blame.

"Darling, are you all right?" St. John asked. "You've gone quite pale."

"Well, she did take that tumble," Diana said.

I tried to shake off my distress. "I'm fine."

At that moment, Mrs. Fairfax called us into the dining room for dinner.

Reading the name cards, I was relieved to find that I was seated between Father Francis and Richard Mason. I hoped I'd get the opportunity to get to know "Uncle Dickie" a little bit and try to determine if he might've murdered Bertha. After all, he was awfully vocal about wanting Edward dead—could it be he wanted his scapegoat gone before anyone discovered the truth about his sister's death?

Our first course was some sort of broth—beef, I think. It was bland, but I was hungry, and it wasn't bad.

"Miss Ingram, tell me about yourself."

I stiffened as soon as Vidocq said the words *Miss Ingram*, but I realized that rather than being the flirtatious Vidocq, he was being the detective.

"I would answer you in your native tongue, Father, but I know not everyone here speaks French," she said.

"I do," Adele said. "Far better than you, I imagine. Would you like me to recite the poem, *Le Corbeau et Le Renard* by Jean de La Fontaine?"

Lowering my head to hide my smile, I was glad to see that not all traces of the old Adele were gone.

"That won't be necessary," Blanche said. "And it would be rude for you to recite a poem when I've yet to answer Father Francis."

Adele shrugged. "Suit yourself. Do you know the poem? It's about a crow who is tricked by a flattering fox."

Blanche pinned her eyes on Richard Mason until he noticed her.

"Eat your soup before it gets cold, my pet," he said to Adele.

She beamed at him, smirked at Blanche, and then dug her spoon into the soup.

"Thank heavens I've been spared the necessity of becoming a governess," Blanche said. "I don't know that I'd have the patience to accommodate some beastly imp under my tutelage."

Adele swallowed and then opened her mouth to speak, but she resumed eating her soup after getting a nudge from Richard.

"I'm confident some man will sweep you off your feet soon, Miss Ingram." Father Francis grinned. "I am available to perform matrimonial services, in case anyone is interested."

Blanche peeked at Richard from under her lashes.

That was subtle.

"Thank you for the offer," St. John said.

I felt my eyes grow wide, looked down, and shoved a spoonful of broth into my mouth.

"I'm sure Jane would adore it if our marriage were to be officiated by her dear friend," he continued.

"As lovely as that would be, we should wait until the sadness of this week has passed, *non?* I should have been more considerate in my speech and will endeavor to be more sensitive."

Once again, I was grateful for Vidocq's quick thinking. Of course, it was his offer to perform marriages that had caused the alarm in the first place. But then, I knew he was only trying to see if Richard Mason would rise to the bait. He hadn't. Did he not return Blanche's feelings? After all, the couple *had* arrived together.

"Mr. Mason, will you be staying on for a little while after the—the end of the week?" I asked.

"More than likely. Mr. Briggs is helping me sort my sister's estate and, although I'd wanted to make this a surprise, I'm attempting to secure Adele's guardianship."

Squealing, Adele leapt up from the table and threw her arms around her Uncle Dickie.

Blanche's mouth thinned and both her hands clenched into fists. It was apparent she hadn't known about Richard's plan to adopt Adele, and she was certainly not happy about it.

AFTER DINNER, everyone went into the drawing room to chat. I took Vidocq aside and asked him if he would accompany me into town tomorrow morning.

"*Mais, oui,*" he said quietly. "I'll secure a carriage, and we will go before the rest of the household begins to stir."

"Thank you."

He cast a discerning eye around the room. "Be careful tonight, *ma petite.*"

"You, too."

St. John strode over to the corner to join us. "What are you two whispering about?" The question was asked good-naturedly, but I felt an undercurrent of possessiveness in his tone.

"I don't want to be rude, but I'd like to go on up to

bed," I said. "Father Francis believes everyone will understand, given my accident earlier today."

"Of course! I'll walk you upstairs." St. John took my arm and ushered me to the center of the room. "Jane needs to retire. Her fall has taken a toll on her, and she needs her rest. She'll see us all at breakfast tomorrow morning."

No, I probably wouldn't, Reader, but he didn't need to know that—and neither did anyone else in that room apart from Vidocq.

Taking a candlestick from the sideboard before we mounted the steps, I lit the candle in it and carried it in the hand not tucked into St. John's arm. I wasn't sure if he was being solicitous or domineering. Feeling it was in my best interest to encourage the man, I squeezed his arm and smiled at him.

At my bedroom door, I let him give me a kiss on the cheek. I wondered how scandalous that was. Since we were engaged, I supposed it was okay.

"Goodnight," I told him.

"I'll be right down the hall should you need me," he said. "Call out, and I'll hurry to your aid."

Good to know. "Thank you."

I opened the door and stepped inside. As St. John turned away, I closed the door, stepped over to my dresser, and lit the other candles in my room.

A silverfish scurried out from under the bed and beneath the door.

Reader, do you have any idea how much that freaked me out?

Were there others? Was the small silverfish a sign that someone—one of *the silverfish*—was hiding somewhere in my room? I got down on my knees and looked under the bed, careful not to set the bedspread on fire—although had someone been hiding there, a fire would have been the least of my worries. Fortunately, there was no person. Also, no silverfish. At least, not under the bed.

I checked the wardrobe. No one there either, but my clothes had been disturbed. Only slightly, but I could tell. The items on my dressing table had been moved too. Someone had searched my room. But for what?

Placing the candlestick on the dressing table, I felt around for panels that might open up and lead to a secret room or hallway. I hadn't had the opportunity to check the area near the staircase yet, but I would.

Unable to find a panel leading to another possible hiding place, I pushed the dresser in front of my door before undressing down to my chemise. I hadn't seen any other silverfish in my room, but the terrifying thought that the silverfish could morph into the persons they were pretending to be gave me serious misgivings about going to sleep as I slid between the sheets.

CHAPTER 8

As I was getting dressed the next morning, I heard footsteps in the hallway. I quickly finished buttoning my blue day dress and walked toward the dresser, intending to push it aside and open the door. Before I could move the dresser, there was a light tap on the door. Then the knob turned.

"Who's there?" I asked sharply.

"*Moi.* Vidocq. Is your door jammed?"

"No." I shoved the piece of furniture out of the way.

Vidocq peeped into the room and then tapped his temple with his index finger. "Smart."

"I thought it couldn't hurt." I frowned. "Unless I needed to get out of here in a hurry."

"Are you ready? The carriage is waiting outside."

We quietly made our way downstairs where I could hear the kitchen staff hard at work. I ventured a glance toward the servants' hallway, but Vidocq took my arm and propelled me out the door.

Dampness soaked through my shoes as we hurried through the dewy grass to the carriage. The horse stamped impatiently on the tarmac.

In the carriage on our way toward town, I breathed a sigh of relief at having gotten out of Thornfield Hall without attracting any notice.

"You let out the breath now, but what will you tell old Sinny Jinny when we get back?" he asked.

"I'll tell him the truth—that it was imperative that Father Francis see Edward, or vice versa, as soon as possible." I opened my reticule, took out a stick of vanilla candy, broke it in half, and gave a piece to Vidocq. "St. John's presence in the house is already smothering me. I feel like if I come to a sudden stop, he'll bump into me."

"Yes, I noticed he is like a puppy following you everywhere."

"I don't like it. I appreciate my independence and autonomy. Had he caught us this morning, I'm sure he'd have insisted on coming into town with us."

"Have you considered the possibility he could be Bertha's killer?" he asked.

I opened my mouth to protest, but Vidocq lifted a finger.

"By getting rid of Bertha Rochester and framing Edward, St. John would not only eliminate his romantic rival, but he would solve the problem of Adele as well." He leaned back against the seat and folded his hands across his middle. "After Edward's execution, all will be tidy for you to marry him and go to India."

"But St. John is a minister."

He winked. "As am I, *ma petite.*"

"Yes, but no one is accusing you of murder," I said.

"No, but I am not what I appear to be—at least, not to most."

I bent forward.

"Ah." He grinned. "My charms have overtaken you at last, *n'est-ce pas?*

"No, but I can't risk our being overheard. Is everyone in Literatia either a literary character or a silverfish, except us?"

"I *am* a character."

I chuckled softly. "I know that. But—"

"You misunderstand. I have been written about widely—both in nonfiction and in fiction."

My smile fading, I asked, "Then how do you know what's going on? Who I am? That I'm not Jane Eyre?"

"Because I am Vidocq. Always and everywhere. I exist outside the world of *Jane Eyre* and all the rest." He dipped his head toward mine. "The shopkeepers you'll meet in town—most of them, anyway—do not realize you are pretending to be someone you are not because you are of little consequence to them. They're minor characters in either this or another story, and to them, you are merely another customer." His mouth turned down at the corners. "You don't need to concern yourself that they are silverfish or wish you harm."

"About the silverfish—how do they operate?" I told him about the one I'd seen in my room the night before.

"Sometimes, *ma petite*, a silverfish is simply that—a bug. It is doing silverfish things with no malicious intent. But other times, these lone silverfish you see have fallen from their host. I suspect they might even be left somewhere in order to do reconnaissance, such as the one you saw last night."

"You think the silverfish I saw last night was spying on me?"

"Shh." He raised a finger to his lips. "You're the one who said we must be quiet."

"Sorry," I mumbled.

"But, yes, I imagine the silverfish you saw was on a mission to discover your identity."

"I assumed the silverfish knew I wasn't Jane, but why do they care?"

"If you aren't Jane but are now the heroine of her story, they know you've been sent by the curator to restore order to Literatia."

"All right, then, if they know why I'm here, why don't they simply destroy the book?" I asked.

"It's hard work. If they can destroy the book by ruining the narrative, it's much easier for them than eating it all at once. It is a rather large tome."

"Vidocq." I hesitated so long to ask my question that he had to prompt me to continue. "A thought occurred to me when St. John was telling of our meeting. The Jane

Eyre he described doesn't sound like the heroine of the novel."

"I believe you have already seen that characters can be different in this altered world, *non?*"

"Yes, I have seen that. What I'm wondering—what I'm afraid to even ask—is do you think it's possible that Jane killed Bertha?"

He looked away. That answered my question.

———

WHEN WE WALKED into the prison, the silverfish jailer was there.

Eyes widening, he gasped. "Vidocq! What are you doing here?"

"Father Francis at your service, my good man," Vidocq said. "I'm here to call on Edward Rochester and to take his final confession. May we be allowed visitation now?"

"Both of you?" The jailer regarded them with suspicion. "Do you know who this girl is?"

"*Mais oui,* she is Jane Eyre, governess to Mr. Rochester's young charge, Adele Varens."

The jailer narrowed his eyes. "You are not Father Francis—you are the detective, Vidocq. And she was sent here by the curator."

"You're ridiculous," I said. "And mean." Turning to Vidocq, I continued, "Yesterday, he pinched me and told me I don't belong here."

"While I agree that a delicate young lady ordinarily has no business in a prison, these are extraordinary circumstances," Vidocq said. "But this mongrel should never have put his hands on you. I'll speak with his supervisor over that."

"I shouldn't like you to cause trouble for me." The man looked around as if to make sure the three of us were still alone. "I need this job."

"Very well." Vidocq stiffened his shoulders. "We'll see Monsieur Rochester without further hindrance then. And you will never put your hands on this young woman again."

The jailer nodded, led them to Edward's cell, and returned to his post.

I looked at Vidocq in question, but he shook his head slightly.

"Later, *ma petite*. Good morning, Edward."

"Good morning." Edward looked from me to Vidocq and back.

I went closer to the bars so I could explain. "This is Father Francis." I lowered my voice to a whisper. "He's really the renowned detective, Vidocq, here to help solve your case."

"Marvelous." Edward blew his breath in my face. "How's that?"

"Much improved," I said, with a laugh.

Vidocq scoffed. "Certainly, you can do better than that. Give the woman a proper kiss— or as best you can with those bars between you."

I felt my cheeks flame.

"If you don't kiss her, I will," Vidocq said. "Blowing one's breath in a lover's face…" He shook his head. "That is the most ridiculous thing I've ever seen."

Edward lowered his head, and we managed to press our lips together between the bars. I was surprised at the spark that flared between us. Was it chemistry? Or static electricity?

"All right, we haven't long, so let's get to business," Vidocq said. "Have you any sins to confess? Unless there is a particularly salacious sin you wish to tell me about, let's work on gaining you your freedom. What do you recall about the night Bertha was murdered?"

"I'd been sleeping. I was awakened by the scream."

"Bertha?" I asked.

Shaking his head, Edward said, "No, it was Grace Poole. She screamed upon finding Bertha dead. Come to think of it, she was shrieking nonstop until the rest of the household was roused."

"Did you immediately investigate the source of these histrionics?" All vestiges of Vidocq's usual playfulness were gone.

"No. I knew where the sound was coming from, and at first—thinking it was Bertha having one of her fits—I stayed where I was." He looked down at the dirty floor of his cell.

"No purpose is served by any self-castigation. The woman was dead when Grace Pool found her," Vidocq said. "Tell me what happened next."

Edward raised his head. "When I saw that the sound was unrelenting, I arose, dressed, and hurried up the stairs to Bertha's chamber. There I discovered her lying on her bed in a puddle of blood. Miss Poole knelt weeping by her side. Another maid and a footman were consoling Miss Poole but not doing anything I felt to be truly useful. I sent the footman to town for the doctor."

"*Tres bien*. Who else was in the house the night your wife was murdered?"

"The only guests were St. John Rivers and Richard Mason, Bertha's brother."

"Why was St. John there?" I asked.

"He'd brought Jane back to Thornfield Hall," Edward said. "And he wasn't the least bit happy about it."

"W-why had Jane—left? Was it because she became aware of Bertha?"

"Jane was always aware of Bertha. Still, Edward and Jane were falling in love but knew they could never act on their feelings."

"Not while Bertha was alive," I said softly.

Edward ignored that statement. "As for why Jane left, Adele began saying cruel things."

"Such as?"

"That Jane would never be mistress of Thornfield Hall, that Jane should leave before she was truly an old maid, that Jane was destined to die alone."

"Are you telling me Jane couldn't handle the taunts of a schoolgirl?" I asked.

"It was more than that. Adele's attacks became more

mean-spirited. She put foxglove in Jane's tea one morning. Miss Poole caught her at it and kept Jane from drinking it."

My jaw dropped. "Adele tried to poison Jane?"

"I believe she was intending to make her sick, not attempting to kill her," Edward said.

"Disturbing behavior for one so young, *non*?" Vidocq shook his head. "Remind me not to let that child get too close to my food."

"Okay, now I understand why Jane left," I said. "Why in the world did she come back?"

Edward looked away, and realization dawned on me.

"For you," I said.

"For Edward," he clarified. "Adele had promised to never pull any more pranks—malicious or otherwise—on Jane again. Edward's threat of sending her to Lockwood School scared her straight."

"And how did the wee poisoner feel about Madame Rochester?" Vidocq asked.

"Ambivalent." Edward shrugged. "Adele cared no more about Bertha than she did about any of the scullery maids. In her opinion, the only good thing about Bertha being at Thornfield Hall was that her presence effectuated Richard's visits."

"Why was he at your home on the night his sister died?" Vidocq asked.

"No particular reason other than to visit," Edward said. "He would typically stay at Thornfield Hall a few days every month."

Vidocq nodded. "And what was his relationship with Bertha?"

"I would imagine it to be one-sided. Bertha was incapable of having a true relationship with anyone. The only person who even came close to being able to interact with her was Miss Poole, who'd been with her since Bertha was in her early teens."

"Most interesting." Vidocq rubbed his chin. "I must have a *tete-a-tete* with Miss Poole. But if the brother had no real connection to Bertha, why was he at your home so often?"

"I presume a sense of duty," Edward said.

Vidocq lifted his hand. "In getting to the truth, we presume nothing, *monsieur.*"

CHAPTER 9

As Vidocq and I left the prison, the silverfish jailer averted his eyes. I looked at Vidocq and opened my mouth to speak, but he again shook his head slightly and propelled me out the door to the carriage.

We were on the road to Thornfield Hall when I asked him why the jailer had adopted such a deferential attitude toward us.

"Silverfish aren't supposed to call attention to themselves. Most people are afraid of them—even the weaker ones like the jailer."

"Wait—these silverfish have a hierarchy?"

He nodded. "The jailer is a lesser silverfish. Mrs. Fairfax is a greater silverfish—she has no one at her post, Thornfield Hall, to whom she must report, and there are lesser silverfish there who must report to her."

"Who?" This worried me. "The only one I'm aware of is Mrs. Fairfax."

"A couple of the maids, one of the footmen—you'll see them soon enough."

I leaned back and tugged at my collar. "Is there some supreme overlord of the silverfish?"

"There is a council," Vidocq said. "They make all the major decisions."

"And what if one of the lesser silverfish incurs the wrath of this council?" I asked.

"Then the conglomerate of silverfish making up that identity would be dismembered, leaving each of the individuals vulnerable."

This was a lot to take in. "So, wait. Is it possible the silverfish I saw in my room last night was an individual that had been decommissioned?"

"*Oui*, but most likely it was there to see what it could learn about you."

"What if I'd stepped on it?" I asked.

Vidocq grinned. "Then I imagine, *mademoiselle*, it would be squished on the bottom of your shoe."

WE RETURNED to find the Adele and the guests having breakfast. St. John got up from the table and came to me at once.

"Darling, I was quite concerned when you didn't come down to breakfast, especially since your accident yesterday." He ushered me to the table and pulled out a chair. "Where have you been?"

I sat down. "Father Francis and I went to visit Edward."

"Why—"

"St. John!" Diana interrupted her brother. "You haven't even greeted Father Francis." She gave Vidocq a broad smile. "You must have some ham and eggs." She began ladling food onto his plate.

"Yes, well, good morning, Father Francis," St. John said.

Vidocq nodded, but he was intent on those ham and eggs Diana was dishing out.

"Why did you go so early?" St. John's attention was back on me. Yay. "Why didn't you wait for me to accompany you?"

"That was my fault," Vidocq said. "I have forever been an early riser. I arose this morning with my heart burdened by the thought of Monsieur Rochester alone as he counts down every dreadful second to his execution." He sighed and shook his head. I imagined he was inspired by the ham. "When I found Jane also up and ready to face the day, I invited her to go along with me fearing *monsieur* wouldn't agree to speak with me otherwise. I am, after all, a stranger to him."

Reader, I half expected him to stand and take a bow. If he had, I'd have applauded.

"And how did you find Edward this morning?" St. John asked.

"As well as can be expected, all things considered." Vidocq dived back into his breakfast.

"I've also been planning to visit Edward." St. John fiddled with his napkin. "I might go later today or tomorrow."

Since I could feel his eyes boring into the side of my head, I turned and gave him a polite response. "That would be lovely, St. John. I'm sure he would be grateful."

Would Edward be grateful about seeing St. John? I kinda doubted it. I didn't know why St. John bugged me as much as he did. You'd think I'd be glad to have someone so obviously on my side here in Literatia. But maybe that was it—I didn't know whether he truly *was* on my side. The only people I felt comfortable trusting were Vidocq and Edward.

Edward. That brief vanilla-scented kiss. I wasn't aware that my lips had curved into a slight smile until Diana called me on it.

"Someone has a look of happiness on her face," she said. "What are you thinking about, Jane?"

It took me a second to realize that she was talking to me—I was Jane. How would Jane answer that question? Especially when she'd just come back from seeing her— what?—employer at the prison where he is awaiting his demise. I decided I couldn't go wrong with a quote from the book.

"'There is no happiness like that of being loved by your fellow-creatures and feeling that your presence is an addition to their comfort.'" I added my own two cents for context. "I'm so glad we're all here to console Mr. Rochester in his time of need."

St. John beamed. "What a wonderful wife you'll make me. How well you will adapt to the mission field."

I gulped down a swig of my tea so I wouldn't have to respond to that.

"What do you say to a walk in the garden after breakfast?" Diana asked. "Just us girls."

"Sounds great," I said.

Mary shrugged her shoulders.

"I need to study," Adele said. "Uncle Dickie, will you help me?"

"Of course, my sweet."

"I'd be happy for some fresh air," Blanche said, trying to smile but looking more as if she were baring her teeth. Anyone could see she wasn't at all happy with Adele monopolizing Richard's time.

The mingling scents of the roses and lavender floated along the garden path adding another level of dreaminess to this adventure. It was as if I'd accepted that my being here was real—but not entirely. I still expected to wake up any moment in my bed in North Carolina and call to laugh about this absurd nightmare with my friend, Connie.

I imagined Connie would look at me like I was crazy if I tried to tell her about Literatia. I wondered what she was doing now. If it was as early there as it was here, she was still in bed with her black cat, Sebastian, on the pillow next to her. Connie was the only person back home that I kept in touch with.

Back home. Would I ever get there? Or would I be stuck here forever?

"Father Francis is a charming character," Diana said, drawing me out of my reverie. "Where did you say you found him?"

"In town." I smiled and decided to lead the conversation away from the detective. "I trust everyone slept well last night."

Mary scoffed. "Listen to Miss Lady of the Manor. You never held that title, and you never will."

I squinted to see if I could detect any silverfish in her teeth. I couldn't. Apparently, this Mary was just mean.

"Mary, Jane was simply asking how we slept," Diana said. "She was being courteous." She gave me a pointed look. "I slept well, thank you."

"I did too," Blanche said, "once I finally dozed off." She sighed. "What do you ladies think about Adele's fascination with Richard? Don't you feel it's a bit strange? They aren't truly related after all, so why should he take over her guardianship?"

Just as Mary wasn't mild and sweet-tempered, this version of Blanche lacked the self-assurance of her novelized counterpart. But since I had little knowledge of Adele's relationship with her "Uncle Dickie," I didn't offer an opinion.

"It's obvious Richard has some paternal affection for the poor child," Diana said. "He likely took pity on her when he saw that she was as alone as his sister was— before you arrived, Jane."

"Or he might be an opportunist," Mary said. "If he could wind up with his sister's inheritance and Adele's as well, he'd be an extremely wealthy man."

Blanche's face hardened. "Neither Richard nor I lack money, Miss Rivers."

"And yet there's no wedding ring on your finger, is there?" Mary smirked.

"Nor is there one on yours," Blanche said. "But, at least, I do have prospects."

"Tell yourself what you must, dear. I'm going back inside." With a sniff, Mary turned and started toward the house.

"Let's hope that black cloud goes with her." Diana shook her head. "I apologize for my sister's disagreeable attitude."

"You've absolutely nothing to be sorry for," I said. "Perhaps she can go sulk with Adele. I believe the only time I've seen that child perk up is when Richard arrived."

"Maybe what you said is right," Blanche told Diana. "Richard saw how despondent the child was and befriended her."

Diana patted the lovely woman's arm. "Imagine what a wonderful father he'll be."

Blanche brightened. "He will be, won't he? And I'm sure he's merely waiting until after Edward's execution to propose."

"Naturally."

"Were Richard and Bertha close?" I asked. Even

though Edward had told me they weren't, I was fully aware that men weren't as likely to share their feelings with each other the way they would with a lover. "Does he speak of her to you often, Blanche?"

"Not anymore," she said. "And I don't speak about her unless he does because I don't want to grieve him. I believe Bertha was always…troubled. But, yes, the two of them appeared to have a bond. He was ever so protective of her. I believe that's why he's outraged by her death—he feels he should have done more to prevent it."

"Does Richard consider it possible that someone other than Edward could have murdered Bertha?" I asked.

"Of course not." She looked at me as if I were stupid. "There was a note. Bertha wrote it to implicate Edward in case she should die a violent death."

"But how can anyone know whether it was actually Bertha who wrote the note?" I tried to keep my tone light but obviously failed.

"What are you implying?" she demanded.

"Edward might have been framed for a crime he didn't commit." I stiffened my back and raised my chin. "An innocent man is about to be executed."

"So says you." Blanche readjusted her light shawl around her shoulders. "At the risk of parroting Mary Rivers, tell yourself what you must. I'm going in out of the sun now. Enjoy the rest of your stroll, ladies."

Diana waited until Blanche was out of earshot. "You're truly convinced of Edward's innocence?"

"I am. The man has been convicted and is days away from the hangman's noose. If he had anything he wished to confess, he had ample opportunity to do so this morning when Father Francis and I visited him."

"He didn't." It was a statement rather than a question.

I shook my head. "I've promised him I'll find Bertha's killer and save him from the gallows."

"Oh, Jane, darling." She hugged me. "I hope you'll be able to keep that promise—I really do."

The phrase *but I wouldn't count on it* was unsaid but strongly implied.

She held me at arm's length. "I'll help you in any way I can—you know that. But you need to marry St. John and go with him to India. It's for the best."

CHAPTER 10

I lingered outside for a few minutes after Diana returned to the house. I knew I had a lot to do to solve Bertha's murder and that I should be inside questioning the guests, but I also needed to catch my breath for a moment. It was tough living this lie—pretending I was Jane Eyre, acting as if St. John was my fiancé, hoping I wasn't the one who murdered Bertha because of my love for Edward. Because what if I was? If I learned I was guilty, I couldn't let Edward hang for my crime. Cooper was concerned about Edward being hanged and the novel being forever altered, but the same would be true— perhaps even more so—if the titular character were hanged. I mean, Cooper could take *me* out of the book; but Jane Eyre would still be guilty and executed for the crime. Right?

Looking down at the wildflowers along the path as I

made my way back to Thornfield Hall, I didn't see St. John approaching.

"Hello, darling. I was getting concerned about you. Is everything all right?"

I nodded. "I have a lot on my mind, that's all. I'm convinced of Edward's innocence, and I'm troubled by the fact that Adele doesn't seem to care at all that Edward is facing the gallows in a matter of days. Doesn't it strike you odd that the child has no apparent affection for her benefactor?"

"Adele *is* only a child," he said. "It's likely she doesn't fully understand the situation well. I suppose that could be a blessing in a way, don't you?"

"I suppose so." I thought Adele understood the situation perfectly but that she simply didn't care, the little psycho. "What is everyone else doing?"

"Mary went up to her room for a rest, and Father Francis is regaling everyone else in the salon with stories from his youth."

"We should join them," I said.

"Of course, but before we do—" He swept me toward a corner of the house where we wouldn't be easily seen from the windows and lowered his mouth to mine.

The kiss wasn't unpleasant, but it lacked the spark I'd felt when Edward had brushed his lips against mine. I wondered if that was because Edward and Jane were in love, but that made no sense. I wasn't Jane. I was Gia. Jane was someone I currently resembled, but my thoughts and feelings were my own. And Edward wasn't Edward.

Before St. John could kiss me a second time, I tucked my chin. "What would people think?"

He laughed. "They'd likely think I was a smart man to be kissing my love. I'm delighted by your modesty, but I can hardly wait until you're my wife."

"Mrs. Jane Rivers." I tried out the name, mainly because I didn't know what else to say. "It has a pleasant ring to it."

"I agree." He tucked my hand into the crook of his arm and led me inside to the salon.

Vidocq arched a brow at me when St. John and I walked into the room. I gave him a slight shrug, and he winked. I couldn't help but smile. He was such an imp.

It still surprised me how, over the course of his life, he'd gone from privileged youth to criminal to the world's premier private detective. Talk about your prodigal son!

And now here he was with me in the salon at Thornfield Hall helping me unravel the mystery of who murdered Bertha Mason Rochester. What were the odds? Astronomical. I wouldn't be surprised if I were to awaken in the hospital and be told I'd hit my head and had been in a coma for the duration of my time in Literatia.

St. John led me over to the sofa where I sat beside Diana. She smiled at me before turning her attention back to Vidocq—or, rather, Father Francis.

Adele was sitting on the arm of a chair occupied by Richard. Blanche sat to their right, her eyes cutting slits into the doting man and the besotted child, who were seemingly oblivious to her glares.

Mr. Briggs came in from the kitchen with a glass of something brown as Father Francis continued his tale of the robber who once convinced the "famous and oh-so-very-clever detective Vidocq, who was in disguise as a fellow robber—to go to the detective's house, wait for the man to come outside, and kill him."

My eyes widened. Was it wise for Vidocq to be telling these people he was investigating that he was a master of disguise?

"Vidocq told me himself," Father Francis said, "that he nearly froze to death lying in wait in the bushes near his own home waiting for himself to come outside!"

Adele laughed so hard she fell against Uncle Dickie's shoulder.

At that moment, I could see a glimpse of the child from the original story. I hoped that if—*when,* I couldn't afford to doubt—all was made right in the world of *Jane Eyre,* all the characters would return to normal. I hated seeing Adele, Mary, and Mrs. Fairfax being such horrible perversions of themselves.

Diana joined in the laughter. "Father Francis, did the robber ever discover the truth?"

"Not that I'm aware," he said.

"That Vidocq must be quite a chap," Richard said. "Is he still living?"

"To the best of my knowledge, that fine fellow is as vibrant as ever." He looked at me. "My dear Jane, could we have a word in private?"

When I said, "Of course," he excused us both from the rest of the party.

We went down the hall to Edward's study, and Vidocq closed the door behind us. Before speaking, he looked all around—up at the ceiling, down at the floor, on the furniture. He put his finger to his lips instructing me not to speak either. I realized he was looking for silverfish.

Even when he became convinced the coast was clear, Vidocq still kept his voice down. "I've learned that Mary is afraid that if Edward is exonerated, Jane won't quit her job, marry St. John, and go to India."

Frowning, I said, "She didn't seem all that concerned about her brother's happiness to me."

"She's not. She's afraid that if Jane won't marry him, St. John won't go to India, and she's desperate for him to leave England. She wants to find a husband, but she despises the men St. John will consider for her."

"Why can't she choose for herself?"

"You must remember she's living in a different time and a different world from the one you're from," he said, displaying a wider knowledge of the world outside Literatia than I was aware he had.

"Okay, that's fair. I'm guessing that if St. John leaves, she'll be able to marry whomever she likes?"

"Right. At least, it would be easier for her if he was out of protesting range."

"What about Diana?" I asked.

"St. John approves of her suitor. Diana believes the man will propose to her soon. She's the one who wants Jane to marry St. John because she wants her brother to be happy."

"She's really wonderful."

"Yes, well, don't put blinders on where any of these people are concerned, *ma petite.* One last thing—Grace Poole felt compelled to confess to me that she often left Bertha to her own devices. She said it was frustrating to sit with Bertha day in and day out and take the verbal and sometimes physical abuse Bertha threw at her."

"I can imagine. In the original novel, Grace drank a lot of gin."

"Grace indicated that Bertha had her good and bad days. On good days, she was lucid and manageable. On the bad days, when she was in the throes of her madness, she seemed to hate everyone and everything. What's more, after hearing Grace describe the woman's behavior, I'm not convinced she was as mad as she pretended to be."

"You think she was faking?" I asked.

"Perhaps not entirely, but I believe she used her condition to manipulate those around her. If, as you suspect, Bertha was having an affair, she could have had an episode of violent behavior to drive Grace away when she wished to be alone with her lover."

"Do you think Bertha committed suicide?"

He rubbed his chin. "Had the woman died from

poisoning, I'd have absolutely believed she'd taken her own life, but I don't accept that she would cut her own throat. The act was performed without fear or hesitation—poor Grace said Bertha's head was nearly completely severed."

I shuddered. "Whoever killed her must've utterly despised her." I had a thought. "Wait, I'd heard Bertha was stabbed but not that her throat had been cut."

"I imagine those speaking with you didn't wish to cause you undue alarm."

"Undue alarm." I nodded, closing my eyes.

Vidocq patted my shoulder. "I don't think Jane Eyre could have done such a thing."

"You don't *think*, but you don't *know*."

"Do you reckon Edward Rochester could love a woman who could be so depraved?" he asked.

"I don't know." I opened my eyes and looked at him through my tears. "I don't know any of the people here, not even the one I'm claiming to be."

"Yes, you know one person. You know Vidocq. We will figure this out."

LATER THAT AFTERNOON, I went in search of Grace Poole. I had no intention of betraying Vidocq's confidence, but I felt Grace might be ripe for some further interrogation after baring her soul to Father Francis.

Before I could find Grace, I discovered Adele in the

library working on the embroidery sampler.

I went into the room and took a closer look over her shoulder at the work. "That's beautiful."

"Thank you. I plan to replace all of these dark, ugly furnishings with pretty things once Thornfield Hall is mine." She looked wistful. "Well, mine and Uncle Dickie's."

"How did the two of you become so close?" I wondered whether Richard had true affection for the child or if he was simply an opportunist who was attempting to secure the wealth of both Bertha and Edward. If the latter, he'd have an excellent motive for murdering Bertha and pinning the crime on Edward.

Beaming, Adele said, "Uncle Dickie has always adored me, telling me I'm like the daughter he has always wanted." Her smile faded. "I know that sniveling Blanche hopes to get her hooks into him, but I'm determined not to let that happen."

"But if your Uncle Dickie loves Blanche, won't that hurt him if you keep them apart?"

"He doesn't love her." She scoffed. "He's under the impression I need a mother, but I don't. I've never had one, and I'm not about to allow some interloper to pretend to care about me so that Uncle Dickie will marry her."

"You don't imagine she could feel real affection for you?" I asked.

"Even if she does, she isn't necessary. All Uncle Dickie and I need are each other."

CHAPTER 11

I mulled over Adele's words as I left the library to continue looking for Grace. While Adele's attraction to Richard could be innocent enough and easily explained —she was an orphan desperate for parental attention—I was suspicious of his affection for her. Sure, he might be a super nice guy who simply felt sorry for the child and took her under his wing; but he didn't strike me as a super nice guy. In fact, he seemed like a jerk toward everyone except Adele. He wasn't even overly nice to Blanche...which begged the question of why she was hanging around with him.

Nearing the dining room, I heard two voices—male and female—speaking in hushed but angry tones. I poked my head inside the room and saw Blanche and Richard standing by the sideboard.

Speak of the devils...

"Excuse me," I said, giving them a vacuous smile. *No,*

of course, I didn't hear you guys arguing. "I'm looking for Grace Poole. Do either of you know where I might find her?"

"No idea," Richard said, barely sparing me a glance before turning toward the window in an un-super-nice-guy fashion.

"I'm sorry," Blanche said. "I have no idea where she could be."

"Thank you." I left with a solid—or at least half-formed—plan to seek each of them out later to see if I could learn what they were arguing about. I had a strong guess, but their answers might provide some insight into Richard's motives with regard to Adele. I truly hoped he had the child's best interests at heart, but those dollar signs in his eyes could certainly impair his vision.

I recalled what Blanche had said about both she and Richard being independently wealthy. But then, what was that verse in Proverbs?

The leech has two daughters. 'Give! Give!' they cry. [Prov. 30:15-16 NIV]

Just because neither of them needed money didn't mean they didn't want it.

Thinking perhaps Grace was cleaning the rooms, I went upstairs and knocked on the door of the first guestroom. When I got no answer, I opened the door.

Mary lay on her side fully dressed atop the coverlet on her bed. She was facing away from the door, but I could see through the mirror on the dressing table that she was clutching an embroidered handkerchief and that she'd been crying.

I quietly closed the door and moved closer to the bed. "Mary?" Although her eyes were open, I spoke softly, hoping my voice wasn't too jarring. "Are you all right?"

She sniffled. "Do I bloody look all right?"

"No. It's obvious you've been weeping, but are you physically ill? Should I have someone come up—"

"Don't do that." She rolled over onto her back. "I'm not hurting anywhere except my heart, and it isn't hurting in the physical sense."

Sitting on the edge of the bed, I asked, "Do you want to talk about it?"

"Not to you," she said. But then she obviously changed her mind. "I know my brother is a good and honorable man. I know it because people ram that fact down my throat every chance they get." She blinked back fresh tears. "But why then does he treat me so harshly?"

"What has St. John done to you? I'll ask him to rectify his behavior at once."

My words seemed to thaw Mary toward me—at least a little.

"There's a man in the village, a widower, who wants to marry me. St. John says the man is too old to raise a family with me. Since St. John believes the only reason to get married is to have children, he has forbidden me to marry this man." She dabbed her wet eyes with the handkerchief. "But I love him, Jane. Whether we have a family or not, I want to live with him and care for him as his wife and his companion."

"I understand completely, and I'll speak with St. John on your behalf, I promise."

She ranted on as if I hadn't spoken. "Not that *he* has always exercised the soundest judgment himself. He came here and counseled that madwoman in the attic for months despite Diana and my telling him it would damage his reputation."

"What? St. John came *here*? To Thornfield Hall?" I felt as if a sliver of ice was snaking down my spine. "I don't recall that."

"It started while you were at Gateshead caring for your dying aunt."

I frowned. "I didn't even know St. John then."

"His coming here had nothing to do with *you*," she said. "He thought he could exorcise the woman's demons or pray the madness out of her or some such nonsense. We told him his reputation would be ruined if he kept visiting Bertha Rochester alone in her bedchamber no matter what he *claimed* he was doing there."

"Right." I stood and began backing out of the room. Had St. John's intentions been honorable? Or was he the man with whom Bertha had been having an affair? My need to speak with Grace was more urgent than ever. "I'll let you rest now, Mary, and I'll see you at lunch."

Lunch.

Maybe Grace had been roped into helping out in the kitchen since there were guests at Thornfield Hall. I hurried back downstairs and darted into the servants' hallway leading to the kitchen. What I saw there brought me to an abrupt halt.

Grace was lying on the floor. Her bulging eyes were wide and aimed heavenward, but they no longer saw anything. Her lips were blue, and the bruises at her throat were becoming darker with every second.

Uh-oh, Reader. Grace Poole had been murdered.

I'D FINALLY CONVINCED ST. John that I'd be fine with Father Francis while he attended to his sisters. As soon as his back was turned, Vidocq and I slipped out into the garden by ourselves.

"What do you make of Grace's murder?" I asked him.

"She obviously knew too much." He took a slight pause. "Did you kill her?"

"Me? No!"

He put a finger to his lips. "Not so loud, *ma petite.*"

"Why would you even ask me that?"

"If you didn't murder poor Miss Poole, then Jane Eyre is not our culprit, *n'est-ce pas?*"

"Not necessarily," I said. "I know what *I've* done, not what Jane has done."

Vidocq patted my cheek as if I were a child. "*Ma petite,* if Jane murdered Bertha, no one else would have a motive to kill Miss Poole, is that not correct?"

"That's true." I considered his statement. "Unless the two events are not connected."

"But of course, they are connected. Why else would the unfortunate woman be found strangled to death such a short time after bearing her soul to Father Francis?"

My eyes widened. "You're right. You have to leave here. If the killer thinks you know his or her identity, you've got a target on your head."

"Bah! Vidocq never runs from the danger. In fact, I embrace it."

"Yeah, well, it might embrace you back this time," I said. "You aren't as young as you used to be."

He pursed his lips and narrowed his eyes. "I will believe that you had no intention of insulting Vidocq." Lifting his chin, he asked, "But am I to understand you no longer wish me to help you?"

I took his right hand in both of mine. "Of course, I want your help. But I could never forgive myself if any harm came to you."

His face softened. "I am the wily old fox, *ma petite*. I will be fine. Let us discuss the matter of most importance before we are disturbed—three of our previous suspects may now be eliminated: Jane, Adele, and Miss Poole, who undoubtedly did not strangle herself to death."

Nodding, I said, "I agree that Adele wouldn't have the strength to murder Grace Poole in that fashion, and we can also eliminate Mary Rivers because I'd just been up in her room with her before I found Grace. In fact, Mary confided something interesting to me." I told Vidocq about St. John coming to visit Bertha. "That's one of the things I wanted to speak with Grace about. Did you have eyes on anyone at the time of her murder?"

"Sadly, no. I was alone in the library. But, Gia, you must be extremely cautious with St. John. And don't—"

When he stopped speaking, I followed the direction of his eyes to see St. John walking toward us.

Vidocq smiled. *"Mon ami,* how are your sisters?" he asked, when St. John was near enough to hear.

"They are shaken but have taken some laudanum and are resting."

"I'm glad," I said. "Mary was distraught to begin with. I was with her before I discovered Grace."

"Yes, well, it's apparent I must take them and you and leave Thornfield Hall as soon as they awaken." He pinned Vidocq with his stare. "Do you not agree that it's dangerous for the women to be here, Father Francis?"

"I don't agree." I anchored my hands to my hips and glared up at St. John. "For one thing, I'd never leave Adele in a house with a murderer."

"Then we'll take the child with us."

Continuing as if he hadn't spoken, I said, "And secondly, I believe we now have evidence to get Mr. Rochester's judgment set aside. I must go inside and talk with Mr. Briggs."

As I tried to move around him, St. John grabbed my arm, his fingers biting into the flesh still bruised and sore from my fall down the stairs the day before. From the corner of my eye, I could see Vidocq white knuckling his cane.

"Let go of me, Mr. Rivers," I said. "I'm not your property yet."

Vidocq tapped St. John's hand lightly with the cane. "No need for more unpleasantness today. Let us revisit this matter when cooler tempers prevail, *non?*"

St. John's jaw clenched, but he released my arm.

I took a deep breath and weighed the decision to storm off against leaving the two men alone together.

Deciding the men's argument might escalate if I left, I wedged myself between the two of them and linked my arms through theirs. "Father Francis is right. We've all had a shock and should go inside and fortify ourselves with a cup of tea."

As we strode up the path toward the house, I barely suppressed a shiver as I wondered where St. John had been when Grace Poole was strangled to death.

CHAPTER 12

When we walked inside, Mrs. Fairfax gave us the once over before saying, "The ones with fortitude are taking tea in the salon."

"Thank you," I said, eager to get to the salon to see who among us had fortitude.

Adele was there, snug against Richard's side. She showed no outward sign of emotion other than clinging to Richard, which wasn't unusual, and I wondered if the Literatia incarnation of Adele was a psychopath. However true that may be, the fact remained that Adele lacked the physical ability to strangle a grown woman.

I had my doubts about Mrs. Fairfax in that regard as well, since she appeared to be old and somewhat brittle, although I supposed that being a silverfish could provide her with additional strength.

In addition to Adele and Richard, Blanche and Mr. Briggs were there in the salon. Mr. Briggs had his back to the room as he stood looking down into the empty grate of the fireplace.

I left Father Francis and St. John to join Mr. Briggs. "How are you?"

"Stunned," he said, turning slightly to gaze down at me. "As is everyone, I'm sure. How are *you*? You're the one who made the grisly discovery."

"It was horrible, to be certain, but at least Miss Poole's murder confims that Edward is innocent. You can get his conviction set aside now, can you not?"

"What?"

I started at Richard's thunderous question. Obviously, I hadn't been speaking as quietly as I'd intended.

"Miss Poole's misfortune has nothing to do with my sister's murder," Richard said.

"I disagree," I said. "Grace Poole was Bertha's closest companion. The fact that Grace's death is also a homicide leads me—and I hope it will persuade the judge—to conclude the two cases are connected. At the very least, Edward deserves a new trial. Don't you agree, Mr. Briggs?"

"I do, Miss Eyre. I plan to submit appeal documents to the court later today."

"That's wonderful." I beamed up at him. "I'll do whatever I can to help."

"I'm merely a poor clergyman," Father Francis said, and I had to clamp my lips together to keep from smiling. "But I'm not convinced that the murder of Grace Poole and that of the mistress of this house are connected."

I knew he must be playing devil's advocate to glean the opinions of others in the room.

"Be that as it may," Mr. Briggs said, "it does give us a tool to work with in prolonging the life of Mr. Rochester. While we await the constable, I'll do research on the legal precedents."

I followed Briggs to Edward's study and closed the door behind us. "Who do you think is responsible for Grace's death? Do you believe her killer and Bertha's are the same person?"

Sitting at the desk, he said, "Truly, I cannot say. What I *can* convey to the judge is that every person who was present at Thornfield Hall when Grace Poole died was on the premises when Bertha Rochester died with the exception of Edward Rochester. I believe that warrants a review of the judgment at least until such time as Miss Poole's murder inquiry is concluded."

I went to peruse the law books on Edward's shelves. "I hope the constable will be here soon." I chose a book and crossed the room to sit on a chair by the window. "Mr. Briggs, how long have you known St. John?"

Briggs had taken out a parchment and a quill, and the quill scratched across the paper before he answered. I felt guilty for disturbing the man while he was trying to exonerate Edward and have him released from prison, but I felt my question was important, and I didn't know when I might get another chance to ask it.

"Not long." He lifted the quill to dip it back into the ink. "I suppose I became acquainted with the young man around the same time you did. That *is* when he began frequenting Thornfield Hall."

"Not according to his sister Mary."

He turned to face me. "What's that?"

"Mary told me St. John visited the house before ever meeting me. She said he came to see Bertha Rochester."

"Whatever for?"

"Mary said St. John thought he could cure Bertha of her madness," I said, "exorcise her demons or something. It's why I was looking for Grace—to ask her about the time St. John spent with Bertha." I opened the book. "You can bet I'll be asking St. John about—"

"Please use the utmost caution, Miss Eyre," he interrupted. "Don't go angering the man."

"Because you believe he might be a killer or because he has asked me to marry him? Why mustn't I anger St. John?"

Frowning, he said, "Dabbling in a man's business is never a wise idea for a young lady."

"But you're certain you never saw St. John here while I was away at Gateshead?"

"No, I don't recall seeing him, although I wasn't here terribly often myself." He turned his attention back to his notes.

As I flipped to the book's Table of Contents, I stewed over what Briggs had said—it was unwise for me to dabble in St. John's business. I knew it was a sentiment of the times in which *Jane Eyre* was written, and although Briggs hadn't answered in the affirmative, I also realized it was safe to assume St. John could be Grace's killer. Before asking St. John about his visits to Bertha Rochester, maybe I should get Diana's take on the situation.

I'd barely made any progress at all in the law book before the constables—there were two of them—arrived to cart away Grace Poole's body and to question all of us. As it was I who had found her, they were particularly interested in talking with me.

Father Francis sat on one side of me, and St. John stood on the other. Mr. Briggs also remained in the room. I felt more than adequately protected. I only hoped neither of the constables was a silverfish intent on hauling me away in chains.

"Miss Eyre, we understand you found Miss Poole lying in the servants' hallway. Is that so?" the younger of the two constables asked.

"It is."

"Why were you in the servants' hallway?" the older man asked, his voice conveying none of the warmth or concern of the other constable.

"I was looking for Grace...er, Miss Poole."

"Why?" he asked.

"Because I wished to speak with her."

"About what?" His voice was hard and relentless. He wasn't about to smile and let me see if there were any silverfish in that face.

"About—"

Vidocq unobtrusively tapped my hand.

Right. I have to be careful.

"About learning to read," I said. "She'd expressed an interest, and I wanted to see if she would like me to teach her when I recommended Adele's classes."

"Why would you teach that woman to read?" St. John asked. Glancing at the constables, he shook his head slightly. "Apologies, gentlemen. Please excuse my outburst."

"No apologies necessary, Mr. Rivers," the older constable who'd taken over the interrogation said. "I'd like to know the answer myself."

Raising my chin, I said, "Everyone has a right to literacy, gentlemen."

READER, it should come as no surprise whatsoever to you whatsoever to learn that I was sent to my room for my outrageous outburst. It was obvious to the men that I was in shock and talking out of my head.

I paced my small chamber like a caged animal, stopping to stomp or to jump up and down occasionally in the vain hope the illustrious menfolk would hear, care, and allow me to return to the salon. If they did hear my tantrum, they likely congratulated themselves on being right about my state of mind.

I gave up, lay down on the bed, and dozed off.

I awoke and, even before opening my eyes, felt that

something wasn't right. I could sense another presence in the room.

Straining my ears, I realized the intruder wasn't merely in my bedchamber, he or she was right beside me. I slightly opened one eye.

"*Bonjour.*"

Vidocq was stretched out beside me on the bed, hands folded atop his chest, and a grin on his cherubic face.

I huffed out a breath of indignation and sat up. "What are you doing?"

"Waiting for you to wake up."

"How long have I been asleep?"

"I don't know," he said. "You were asleep when I got here."

"And it didn't occur to you to wake me up?"

"*Mais non.* You apparently needed a nap."

"But you didn't leave."

"*Vrai.* True. Vidocq stayed to protect you. You are welcome."

"Thank you." A laugh bubbled to the surface. "I really am glad you're here."

He waggled his brows. "Do not think you can have your way with me, *mademoiselle.*"

"Sorry. I'd never presume to take advantage of this situation."

Shaking his head, he said, "I told you not to *think* you can have your way with me. *Know*! Know that you can. Seize the opportunity before you. Vidocq loves a woman who has the confidence."

I laughed again but clapped a hand over my mouth. "What will these people think?"

"Who cares? Most are in such turmoil over Miss Poole's demise, they don't have any idea what's happening elsewhere."

"Good point." I moved to the dressing table to fix my hair. "What have I missed? Are the constables still here?"

"*Oui.* At least, they were when I came upstairs."

"How long ago was that?"

"I would say a quarter of an hour."

Standing to look out the window, I spotted the constables' carriage still outside in front of the house. "Were you able to hear anyone's alibi?"

"Of course. St. John said he was in the garden. Richard and Miss Ingram claimed they were in the dining room, but her demeanor suggested that was not true."

"I saw them in there before I came upstairs and spoke with Mary." I sat back down. "They seemed to be arguing. We need to make a diagram or something to account for the whereabouts of those we're certain of as well as those we're unsure of. I don't—" I stopped speaking when I heard footsteps in the hall. My eyes flew to Vidocq.

He put a finger to his lips and then quietly got up and went to the wardrobe. He climbed inside and closed the door.

I went to the bedchamber door and opened it just as Diana was preparing to knock.

Smiling slightly, I said, "I'm glad it's you. How are you?"

"Concerned about you," she said. "How dreadful for you to have found poor Miss Poole that way."

"It was a horrible shock, but I do feel better after having a rest." I glanced toward the wardrobe, thinking of how uncomfortable poor Vidocq must be. "Shall we take a walk?"

"Yes, I'd like some fresh air."

I grabbed my bonnet and tied it on as Diana and I were walking toward the stairs.

Imagine my surprise, Reader, when I saw Father Francis emerging from his room.

My jaw dropped. How had he done that? He couldn't have gotten out of the wardrobe and past Diana and me without either of us seeing him.

"*Bonjour, mademoiselles.* I feel somewhat restored after my kip. I hope you do as well."

"We do, Father Francis," Diana said. "We're headed outdoors for some fresh air. Would you like to join us?"

"Perhaps I will after I check to see that I'm not needed to offer solace to anyone." He nodded at the stairs. "After you."

I allowed Diana to go ahead of me and turned—still gaping—to Vidocq.

He gently patted the underside of my chin to instruct me to close my mouth, and he winked.

I went down the stairs intent on extracting an explanation from Vidocq as soon as possible.

I was relieved that Diana and I had the garden to ourselves, but I didn't kid myself that our privacy would last. St. John seemed to have a tracking device on me, and I needed to question Diana before he found us.

"Have you popped in on Mary?" I asked, keeping my voice light. "I was with her moments before I found Grace Poole, but to my knowledge, she didn't come downstairs."

"The constables sent for both of us, but she returned to her room as soon as she'd given them her account." She shrugged. "Of course, she didn't know anything—she'd been in her room both before and after the murder."

I wanted to ask Diana where she had been, but I felt St. John's relationship with Bertha Rochester was more pressing. Yet how could I frame my questions in a way that wouldn't offend this woman who was so clearly devoted to her brother?

"Dear St. John." I thought that was a good start. "I never realized he'd tried to help Mrs. Rochester."

Diana stiffened. "Did Mary tell you that?"

"She did; and while I admit she informed me as if St. John had been wrong to offer Mrs. Rochester his help, I believe it was noble and courageous of him to do so."

"Yes," she said. "Yes, it was. I'm relieved to hear you say that. Mary feared St. John's coming here would damage his reputation. But he was more concerned with that poor woman's soul than with his own well-being."

"If she was truly possessed, he could very well have been risking his life attempting to save her," I said.

"He did! More than once, he returned home with scratches."

Scratches, huh? "Did he succeed in providing Mrs. Rochester any relief?" I highly doubted innocent Diana would realize what a loaded question I'd asked.

"Alas, no," she said. "I believe he finally lost hope in his ability to save her."

"I wonder why he never told me he tried," I said.

She linked her arm through mine. "Oh, darling, no man wants the woman he loves to know he failed at anything."

I said nothing, but my brain was manufacturing a least a dozen sarcastic retorts.

As expected, St. John came marching down the path to join us mere seconds after Diana had spoken. No need to wonder how I was going to broach the subject of Bertha Rochester with him—Diana did it for me.

"Mary has been spouting nonsense to Jane about your visits to Thornfield Hall."

"What nonsense?" he asked. "Why wouldn't a besotted man spend time with the object of his affection?" He smiled at me.

I wondered which "object" he was talking about—me or Bertha.

"She was speaking of your visits here before you met Jane," Diana said. "The ones you made while attempting to help Mrs. Rochester."

St. John's face reddened. "Yes, well, Mary is a self-serving woman. She would never consider putting someone else's welfare ahead of her own."

"Were you able to help Mrs. Rochester at all?" I asked with as much naivete as I could muster.

"No, and I don't wish to speak of it further."

"I understand, but I simply—"

"I said I do not wish to speak of it, Jane." His face even redder than before, he informed Diana and me that we were all going back inside now. He stormed off leaving us to trail along in his wake.

I'd have rather remained in the garden out of sheer spite and a refusal to be ordered around, but I was ready to go back inside to see what was going on with the constables and the rest of their suspects.

THE CONSTABLES WERE INTERROGATING one of the scullery maids when I entered the salon. The poor girl was in tears. Could I have been mistaken about Grace's murder? Could her homicide have been a random act unconnected to the death of Bertha Rochester?

No way. I refused to believe that. Besides, Vidocq was of the same mind as I was, and he was much more experienced in criminology.

Mrs. Fairfax stood against the wall, arms folded, watching the exchange between the young woman and the constables with an enigmatic smile on her face.

Moving closer—at least, as close to her as I could bear to be—I asked, "Have they questioned you yet?"

She scoffed. "What do you think?"

I didn't know *what* to think, especially after that response, but Mrs. Fairfax was obviously not going to answer my question. I tried another tactic. "Do you believe this girl is guilty?"

"Only of being a spineless, sniveling little mouse."

I felt something crawling on my neck. Unable to suppress a sharp bark of alarm, all eyes in the room turned to me as I slapped myself. A silverfish fell to the floor, and Mrs. Fairfax snickered.

"This is a private inquiry," the younger constable said to me. "You need to leave."

I stepped out of the room but noticed that Mrs. Fairfax remained. The same rules must not have applied to her.

Wandering down the hall to the library, I found

Briggs, Vidocq, and Adele. Vidocq and Adele were conversing in French as Mr. Briggs perused a thick, brown book. I guessed it was another legal text, but I was unable to see the title to confirm.

As I pulled out a chair to sit across the table from Briggs, I asked him, "Is there anything I can do to assist you? I realize our time is short."

"How is your penmanship?"

The note I'd written for Vidocq at the inn had been legible, so I said, "It's great." Sure, writing with a steel pen or even a quill wasn't easy, but I had a hero to save.

"Excellent. Let's go to Edward's study and draft a letter to the judge straightaway."

AFTER BRIGGS LEFT to deliver the letter, Vidocq and I sneaked outside to compare notes. We didn't go into the garden. St. John was certain to find us there. We found a small bench on the east side of the house.

"The path before us leads to the chapel," Vidocq said, nodding toward a narrow walkway a few feet from where we sat. "Should old Sinny Jinny find us here, we'll say we're on our way to the chapel to pray and ask him to join us."

"Praying in the chapel is actually a good idea," I said. "It might take a miracle to get Edward out of this mess."

"Then we shall go to the chapel after we have compared our findings, *oui?*"

"*Oui*...um, yes. So, was Adele telling you anything interesting?"

"She is angry because Richard and Blanche went into town without her," he said. "I cajoled her by implying perhaps her Uncle Dickie had gone to buy her a present since she'd had such a shock today."

"The child might've had a shock, but I don't feel it had any adverse effect on her. She's awfully cold, don't you think?"

He rubbed his chin. "I'm undecided as to whether she is unfeeling or merely self-absorbed and emotionally immature. She had little—I am guessing—contact with Grace Poole and thus was unmoved by the woman's murder. Same with Bertha Rochester's death and Edward's looming execution—their fates do not directly affect her."

"But they do," I said. "If Edward is executed, her entire existence changes, and I'm not just talking about in the context of the novel."

"In what way will Adele be affected in her own eyes? She will remain at Thornfield Hall, the only home she has ever known with one difference—her guardian will become Richard, and she believes her new situation will be delightful."

"That's true." Maybe Vidocq was right. Maybe Adele was simply selfish and immature rather than a psycho. Maybe. Maybe not. "I spoke with St. John about his visits to Bertha Rochester."

"Did that go over as well as I anticipated it would?" he asked, trying not to laugh.

"If you imagined he'd flat out refuse to speak of his time with Bertha other than to say he was unable to help her, then yes. By the way, Mr. Briggs said he never saw St. John here when I was away at Gateshead—which reminds me, how did you get from my wardrobe to your room without Diana or me seeing you?"

"Many rooms in estates such as these have doors that open into secret passageways used by the servants to offer discretion to their employers, *ma petite*."

"All right, but how did you get to the secret passageway door from the wardrobe?" I asked.

"There is a door in the back of the wardrobe. If you open that door, you'll immediately see another door. Open it, and you are in the passageway." He spread his hands. "Imagine a maid brings clean clothes to your room. She has been instructed not to inconvenience members of the household, so she opens the wardrobe from the passageway and places your clothes inside. You are not disturbed, and she has done her job. *Voila*."

"That's ingenious. And the presence of secret passageways explains so much—not only how Bertha Rochester could have guests come and go from her bedchamber without anyone knowing, but also how I got pulled down the stairs without seeing who did it."

"True. But you are wrong about one thing, *ma petite*. Someone always knows."

CHAPTER 14

Vidocq—or, rather, Father Francis—and I had gone on to the chapel. One, it was a good cover story if anyone should ask where the two of us had been. Two, I'd meant what I'd said about needing a miracle. We were walking back to the house when a carriage arrived.

"Wonder if it's Briggs or Richard and Blanche?" I asked.

"The quarrelsome lovers, I imagine. They have been gone quite a while."

Briggs got out of the carriage, and then Edward stepped out.

I gasped and began to run, ignoring Vidocq's emphatic *non*. Barreling into Edward, I nearly knocked him to the ground as I threw my arms around his waist. "You're home!"

"I'm home." He briefly embraced me and was smiling as he pushed me firmly away from him.

A panting Father Francis joined us and also hugged Edward. "I...too...am... most...happy." He stopped and caught his breath. "Welcome home, *mon ami*. Jane and I were moments ago in the chapel praying for your release. Our joy at the realization of a miracle has made us both forget ourselves."

"Yes. We did. We did forget." I forgot I wasn't a Regency-era governess living under strict Victorian rules of conduct rather than an American who'd been known to embrace strangers following the favorable outcome of a sporting event.

Reader, Briggs likely believed Jane Eyre to be a trollop.

In case it wasn't enough that I'd exposed my wanton side in front of Briggs, there stood St. John when I turned toward the door.

Hurrying over to him, I grasped his hand. "Look! Mr. Briggs was able to get Mr. Rochester released from prison. Isn't that wonderful?"

"It is, unfortunately, a temporary reprieve," Briggs said before St. John had a chance to answer. "The judge has temporarily set aside his previous sentence until the murder of Grace Poole has been solved. Mr. Rochester is currently under house arrest and in my custody until such time as a new trial is ordered or the —" He cleared his throat. "—the sentence has been reinstated."

"But it's something." I released St. John's hand and beamed at Briggs. "Thank you for effectuating Mr. Rochester's second chance."

"Why don't we go inside and have a drink," Edward suggested. "I'm eager to settle into my favorite chair."

"Of course, you are," Father Francis said, "and I'm always ready for a drink."

As we walked inside, another carriage arrived. We turned to see Richard leaping out almost before the vehicle had stopped.

"What's going on here?" He strode toward Edward.

"Mr. Rochester has been granted a temporary stay while the judge awaits the constables' report on Grace Poole's murder," Briggs said.

I glanced at Edward and saw that his face was like flint.

"Richard, I'll remind you *once* that you are a guest in my home." His tone was even harder than his face.

"Uncle Dickie!" Adele burst through the door and grasped one of Richard's clenched hands. "Where have you been? I'm ever so cross with you for—"

"Not now." He jerked his hand away.

She refused to be dismissed. "I'll forgive you if you've brought me a present."

"You'll go inside immediately, or I'll lock you in a closet until you've learned some manners," Richard said.

"You'll do no such thing!" I shouted. Although it was Jane Eyre and not I who'd been imprisoned in the red room at Gateshead because of some minor indiscretion and scared half out of her mind, I was outraged by Richard's threat.

"What—or who—gives you, a mere governess, the

right to behave as if you are the mistress of Thornfield Hall?" Richard asked.

"Miss Eyre is acting as Adele's advocate, which she has every right to do with regard to the role she was hired to perform," Edward said. "Besides being Adele's governess, I'm aware that she cares deeply for the child and is passionate about her safety."

Richard smirked. "I imagine you are aware of many of Miss Eyre's passions."

"How dare you—" St. John began.

"Enough." Briggs held up his hands. "Our tempers are besting us, gentlemen. Let us go inside, have some refreshment, and postpone further conversations until such time as they may be conducted civilly."

"Or not at all." Father Francis grinned. "Now, who must we see about those refreshments?"

Once inside, I followed the weeping Adele to her room. She'd slammed the door shut but didn't object when I opened it.

Sitting on the edge of her bed, I brushed her long dark hair off her face.

"I thought Uncle Dickie loved me!"

"He does," I said, hoping that statement wasn't a lie.

"No, he doesn't! Nobody loves me!"

"I love you." I fully believed Jane loved Adele. In the novel, she and Rochester wound up adopting Adele after they were married, so they both must've loved her.

"Only because you're *paid* to look after me."

"That isn't true. I'd love to have you for a daughter."

She sat up. "You would?"

"Of course, I would. And I'm sure Mr. Rochester and Mr. Mason love you too. Mr. Mason was merely upset before."

Adele sniffled and rubbed her eyes with her fingertips. "You may marry Uncle Dickie and be my stepmother then."

I smiled. "I don't think Mr. Mason likes me very much."

"Then we shall *make* him like you."

We were interrupted by a tap on the door. Blanche stuck her head inside.

Adele flung herself back against her pillows. "Did Uncle Dickie send you?"

"No. But I brought you this." Blanche produced a doll from behind her back. "I got it for you in town." She handed the delicate figure to Adele.

"Thank you." The child briefly examined the doll before looking back at Blanche. "Where is Uncle Dickie?"

"He'll probably be up to see you soon," Blanche said. "I'll go find him and send him upstairs."

"Thank you."

"Meanwhile, you rest." I had my doubts as to whether Richard would climb the stairs to check on Adele after the way he'd acted outside. Once we were out in the hall and out of earshot of Adele, I asked Blanche, "Why is Mr. Mason so thoroughly convinced Mr. Rochester killed his sister? Didn't Grace Poole's murder shine even the slightest doubt on Mr. Rochester's guilt?"

"Not in the least. He's adamant it was Edward who killed Bertha."

"And yet he was a character witness at Mr. Rochester's trial. Don't you find that odd?"

Blanche took a deep breath. "You'll recall Richard was vague in his testimony, saying basically that Edward was a shrewd businessman. He merely wanted to ensure that Edward would entrust Adele's guardianship to him."

"Why is that so important to him?" I asked.

"Because he loves the child, of course. He doesn't want her to be sent away from her home."

"He treated her badly earlier, and I do hope he goes up and apologizes to her."

"I'm sure he will," Blanche said, as she headed for the staircase.

I wasn't convinced Richard was doing as well financially as he'd like everyone to believe. Securing Adele's guardianship would ensure him Edward's money. Had either Edward or Mr. Briggs investigated Richard's financial situation?

As I followed Blanche downstairs, I wondered how I could get Edward to myself. Maybe he could tell me how long it would be before Cooper got us out of Literatia. Would we be able to go home right away now that Edward had been released from jail? Or would we have to solve not only Bertha's murder but Grace's too in order to adjust the novel's narrative back to normal? Also, if Bertha and Grace were murdered by the same person—as was the most likely scenario—wasn't Edward in as much danger here at Thornfield Hall as he'd been in prison?

When Blanche and I went into the salon, only Vidocq —or, rather, Father Francis—was there. He was lounging on the sofa with his eyes closed.

"Perhaps we should go to another room," Blanche said softly.

Father Francis opened his eyes. "I forbid you to leave before you've had your tea."

I noticed the tea tray sitting on the table in front of the sofa and wondered how long it had been sitting there. Was the tea even still hot?

Blanche laughed. "I thought you were sleeping."

"*Mais, non!* I was merely giving my eyes a rest so they could better drink in your beauty, Miss Ingram—and yours as well, dear Jane."

Feeling the pot, I could see it was indeed suitably warm. I refilled Father Francis's cup and said, "Be sure not to burn that silver tongue of yours." I poured Blanche and me a cup as well.

"Did you and Mr. Mason have a pleasant trip into town?" he asked Blanche.

"We did." She tasted her tea. "We went mainly to stay out of the way of the constables. Richard didn't want to impede their investigation."

"Why then did he choose not to take Adele along?" he asked. "Am I correct in believing he wanted the venture to be more romantic?"

Blanche blushed and lowered her eyes.

Father Francis kept talking. "Might we expect an announcement at dinner this evening?"

"Stop teasing her, Father Francis," I said. "You're embarrassing her."

"Perhaps I would simply like to know if I yet have a chance to win the young lady's heart."

"You are too much!" Blanche laughed. "You know, I don't understand why Richard felt so strongly about leaving—we weren't in anyone's way. Perhaps Miss Poole's murder was simply too upsetting a reminder of his sister's recent demise."

"That's probably true," I said. "And it would explain Mr. Mason's anger upon returning to see that Mr. Rochester was home."

"I hope that when he has time to consider the matter properly, Mr. Mason will see the possibility of Edward's innocence," Father Francis said. "The knave who strangled Miss Poole might well have killed Mrs. Rochester too."

"Yes, well, I doubt Richard will ever be persuaded of Edward's innocence." Blanche put her cup on the tea tray. "Excuse me, I'm going to go up to my room for a bit."

Moving closer to Vidocq and lowering my voice, I asked, "Where did Edward go? I'd love to talk with him."

"The last account I had of him, he was visiting the stables. I'll escort you there."

"Thanks. Did I mess up terribly when I hugged him?"

"The gesture most assuredly indicated a lapse in judgment, but given the circumstances, your behavior could be excused," he said. "But be careful how others see you interacting with Edward from here on out. You cannot allow your behavior to damage Jane's reputation or to incite St. John to murder either or both of you. He doesn't seem to care for Edward anyway. Let us not throw whiskey on the bonfire, *n'est-ce pas?*"

Vidocq and I found Pilot before we found Edward. The large black dog loped up to us and allowed me to pet his head. I hadn't seen him before now and supposed it was because his master hadn't been home. The poor dog had likely been waiting for Edward here in the barn.

Stepping into the stables and saw Edward brushing his horse Mesrour's gleaming black coat. The stallion tossed his head and stamped his feet.

"Would either or both of you care to go for a ride?" Edward asked.

Although Jane hadn't ridden in the novel, I was an accomplished rider. "I'd love to."

"Not me." Vidocq leveled his gaze at me. "Remember what I told you, *ma petite.*"

"I will."

After we'd ridden a good distance away from the stables, Edward asked me what Vidocq had meant.

"He told me I needed to be careful not to damage Jane Eyre's reputation with my behavior." I shrugged. "In my day, it isn't a big deal to hug a friend, especially upon his release from jail."

"We do need to be prudent and watchful, but I'm glad for the opportunity to speak with you privately."

"I've been wanting that too," I said. "Tell me everything. When did you get here? Now that you're out of the woods, so to speak—" We were actually riding *toward* some woods. "—will Cooper bring us home soon? How does he do that exactly?"

Edward laughed. "Neither of us safe yet. There's still a death sentence hanging over my head, and the person who killed Bertha and Grace must be found and brought to justice."

"I thought I was sent here to save you."

"And the book," he said.

"How exactly does that work?"

"When the killer is exposed, the novel will right itself and reset at the beginning."

I groaned. "Does that mean Jane will have to go through all that garbage with her mean aunt and cousins again? And that horrible school? But what about the silverfish?"

"Your thoughts really do go a mile a minute, don't they?" Edward shook his head. Once the council sees that the silverfish have failed, they'll be disassembled and reassigned. *Jane Eyre* might not be safe forever, but the narrative will be safe for a while—if we meet our objectives."

"What's your real name?" I asked.

"It's best you don't know it yet. With this being your first assignment, you're liable to slip and call me by the wrong name if you know me as anything other than Edward."

I didn't really feel like that was fair—he knew my real name—but I could see his point. "How long have you been doing this?"

"Quite a while."

"When did you trade places with Edward?"

"Just before Jane went to Gateshead to care for her dying aunt." He directed Mesrour to a nearby stream and dismounted.

As the horse drank, Edward helped me down from my mount.

I meant to ask Edward if he had any idea who killed Bertha and Grace, but the words that tumbled from my lips were, "Were you and Jane having an affair?"

"No." He grinned.

"I apologize for all the questions, but didn't you have a ton of them the first time you found yourself in Literatia?"

"I doubt I had a ton, but probably several hundred pounds' worth. Why do you care whether or not I was having an affair with Jane. Jealous?"

"Of course not. But you kissed me at the jail."

"Father Francis told me to. Besides, that was hardly a proper kiss."

"And what do you call a proper kiss?" I asked.

With a wicked gleam in his eyes, he stepped closer. "Is that an invitation?" He bent his head and kissed me then.

Reader, I kissed that man right back. Yep. I'd been warned to conduct myself like a lady—a Victorian lady—and yet threw myself into Edward's arms the first chance I got. Way to go, Gia!

It was weird, but his kiss made me feel like everything was going to be all right.

"What do we do now?" I asked when he lifted his head. He arched a brow, so I quickly clarified. "To solve the case."

"Someone at Thornfield Hall wants me dead. I imagine he—or she—will take another stab at it since the hangman's noose has been delayed."

"Another *stab* at it? Really?"

He grinned. "I thought I was being clever."

Placing my hand on his arm, I said, "Promise me you'll be careful."

"You have my solemn word."

"You do know about the wardrobes and secret passageways, don't you?"

"I do," he said.

"I didn't until earlier today. I used the dresser to bar my door last night. I don't know how I'll block off the wardrobe, though."

"I can help you with that. I'll come through tonight after everyone else goes to bed."

"But our reputations—"

"Will be fine." He smiled slightly. "I'll use the secret hallway and enter your room through the wardrobe."

"Is that how St. John visited Bertha?"

"I don't know. I was only aware of one meeting between them." Frowning, he asked, "Were there others?"

After telling him what I'd heard from Mary and my later conversation with Diana and St. John wherein he refused to discuss his visits to Bertha, I said, "I intend to ask him later about the button I found. I realize that if it is his button, it doesn't mean much since he has already admitted to being in Bertha's bedchamber, but it might allow me to reopen the conversation."

"Promise me *you'll* be careful."

"I will. But I'm ready for us to be home. Aren't you?"

"More than you know," he said.

I smiled and walked toward my horse. "Then let's catch this murderer."

***

WHEN WE GOT BACK to the stables, Edward and I left the horses in the care of the grooms and went our separate ways. I'd told him I intended to search Grace Poole's room and was on my way to do that when I was stopped by St. John on the garden path.

"Where have you been?"

"I went riding," I said. "I hadn't ridden in ages, and it was refreshing to be on horseback again."

"Did you go with Edward?"

"Yes. Father Frances and I ran into Mr. Rochester in the stables, and he invited the two of us to accompany him." I did my best at making a pouty face. "I'm sorry you weren't there to go with us, but maybe we can go again tomorrow."

"I never knew you to be such an equestrian."

"You still have a lot to learn about me, St. John Rivers."

He chuckled, pulled me closed, and said, "I'm looking forward to discovering your every secret."

"And I'm eager to uncover yours." I took out the button I'd been carrying around since I'd found it. "Are you missing a button, my dear?"

He took it from my palm and examined it. "No, this isn't mine." He handed it back. "Where did you find it?"

"In Bertha Rochester's room."

Eyes narrowing, his smile disappeared as he said, "That's not funny."

"It wasn't intended to be."

"Are you accusing me of something?"

"Of course not. I was simply asking if this button belonged to you. It's a man's button, and you visited Mrs. Rochester's room," I said. "Had it been yours, I'd have been happy to sew it back on for you."

His expression softened slightly. "That's thoughtful. Thank you."

I dropped the button back into my pocket and took his arm. "You don't have to be so defensive and suspicious all the time you know." I started moving in the direction of the house.

"Am I? If I am, it's simply because now that I've found you, I'm determined to never let you go."

"Aw." *We call guys like you* possessive *in my day, St. John.* "Did the constables ask you about Grace Poole?"

"Yes, they spoke with everyone in the house at the time—you know that."

"Sure, but did they specifically ask you anything about Bertha Rochester?"

St. John stopped walking. "Why would they?"

"Well, it's Mary." I hated to throw poor Mary under the bus, but I desperately needed to get into St. John's head. I figured the best way to do that was to make him think I was firmly on his side. "What if she told the constables the same tale—with the same sort of insinuations—she relayed to me? She's horribly upset with you. You should let her marry whomever she likes. Really, St. John, what harm would it do?"

"What insinuations did she make?" he asked.

"By saying she feared for your reputation because you were spending so much time in Mrs. Rochester's bedchamber, she led me to think that perhaps..." I shrugged.

"What kind of man do you think I am?"

"A wonderful man," I said, "but also a human with normal desires."

"My only desire is for you."

"That puts my mind at ease."

Reader, had I been Pinocchio, my nose would have grown two inches and sprouted a leaf.

"I must speak with Mary at once and see that she curbs that wicked tongue of hers," he said.

Patting his arm, I said, "Don't be too harsh with her."

We walked into the house, and as soon as he strode toward Mary's room, I went in search of Grace's room. I truly hoped I hadn't given Mary a death sentence. But if she did wind up dead, we'd know St. John was our murderer, case closed, and Mary would be revived when the book reset itself. Right? I hoped that was right. I didn't want to be responsible for anyone getting hurt.

Before I got to the maids' quarters, an arm encased in a brown sleeve shot out like a shepherd's crook and hauled me into an alcove. Fortunately, I'd recognized the sleeve as belonging to Father Francis and didn't cry out.

"What are you doing? Trying to scare me out of my wits?"

"*Mais non*, but I think you are searching for Grace Poole's room."

"That's exactly what I'm doing," I said. "Would you like to come with me?"

"Ah, Father Frances has been there already. Some of the other servants were glad to have me go into Miss Poole's room and exorcise the evil spirits that might be lingering there following her murder."

"Then you know which room is hers—great. Let's go."

"*Non.*"

"*Non?*" I asked. "Why *non?*"

"Two reasons." He held up an index finger. "To go back would look suspicious." He raised the second finger. "And there is no longer a need to go. I thoroughly searched the bedchamber."

"Did you find anything?"

He reached into a pocket sewn on the inside of the robe and brought out a stack of letters tied with a white ribbon. "*Voila.*"

"I thought Grace was illiterate," I said, carefully taking the letters.

"These are not her letters, *ma petite.*"

My eyes widened, and I gasped as I reached for the end of the ribbon.

"Not here!" He took back the letters. "You Americans —you have none of the patience."

"How did you know I'm from America?" I asked.

"Because you have none of the patience!"

"Well, where are we going to look at these? We need to examine them as soon as possible."

Turning his mouth down at the corners, he asked, "Are you so eager to get rid of Father Francis?"

"What? No. I just want to find out who killed Bertha and Grace and save Edward. Don't you?"

"I do. But when the killer is exposed, I must leave."

Honestly, I hadn't considered how this ordeal would affect Vidocq. He wasn't a character in *Jane Eyre*.

"I'm sorry. I should never have involved you in my

problems. I was afraid and didn't know what to do or where—"

"Hush, *ma petite*. I did not want to make you have the regrets."

"But what will happen to you when this case is resolved—or if it isn't?"

"When I agreed to accompany you on this adventure, I contacted my publisher and postponed our meeting until tomorrow afternoon. If the case is solved by then, I will leave, meet with my publisher, and produce the memoir you will one day read and come to adore Vidocq."

"And if the case isn't solved?" I asked.

"I will still meet with my publisher. Vidocq is not an imbecile."

I laughed.

"That's better," he said. "I will not have you be sad. However, never fear, if there remains a murderer within the walls of Thornfield Hall, I will return the following day to ferret out the scoundrel."

"Deal. Now, where can we read these letters?"

Vidocq and I hurried to the chapel with our purloined letters. It was a good place to find some privacy, plus who could get angry with us for being devout?

Upon stepping inside, Vidocq looked down and stomped his left foot. "A silverfish—*l'espion*."

"A spy?"

He nodded. "I feel we're no longer safe here. We will

divide the letters, read them privately, and confer afterward. *D'accord?*"

"Okay." I handed over half the letters and kissed his cheek. "You can't imagine how thankful I am for your help."

"I am thankful for another opportunity to right a wrong. You make Vid—Father Francis—feel young again. Now let us go to our rooms and read other people's private correspondence."

CHAPTER 16

I sat at my dressing table with my half of Bertha's letters before me. I'd already scoured the room and the wardrobe for silverfish and had slid the dresser in front of my door. There wasn't much I could do about the wardrobe yet, so I merely kept a close eye on it.

Taking the first letter from the stack, I opened it and read:

Dearest Bertha: I'm sorry I upset you upon my last visit to Thornfield Hall. We must put our petty differences aside and be united. I know Edward doesn't treat you fairly. Keeping you locked away like a criminal is wrong. He will one day pay for his actions. I will be back to visit you as soon as I can. Fond regards, Dickie

Interesting. What had Bertha and Richard quarreled about? How far had Richard been willing to go to make Edward pay?

I put the letter back in the envelope and opened the next one.

Sister, I pray this letter finds you well.

The writing was different, but at first, I thought this was another letter from Richard. I read on and learned the letter was from Bertha and Richard's sister.

I write to you today because my health is deteriorating. This will likely be the last missive you receive from me. You will surely be blessed for rescuing me from ruin when Adele was born. She could not have gone to a better home.

I didn't know about that, but I was still reeling from the fact that Adele was actually Bertha's—and therefore Richard's—niece. Did Richard know? That would certainly explain his affection for Adele.

There was a tap on my door, and Diana called, "Jane, darling, it's time for dinner!"

"I'll be right down." I hid the letters under the mattress before moving the dresser back into place and walking down the hall.

Father Francis awaited me at the head of the stairs. "Are you well? Your face is quite pale."

"I've been engaged in some interesting reading," I said. "Some of it rather shocking."

"I have read some surprising things myself," he said.

Despite my eagerness to confer with Vidocq about Bertha's correspondence, I hadn't had any real food to speak of since breakfast. As far as I knew, no one else had either—unless Blanche and Richard had eaten in town.

We entered the dining room to find Adele standing by

the table wearing a cute dress and an expression of triumph. The triumph alarmed me.

"Uncle Dickie, doesn't Jane look nice this evening?" she asked.

I turned to see Blanche and Richard walking behind us.

"She does," he said, "as do you." Apparently remembering there were other women present, he added, "Blanche and the Rivers sisters look lovely as well."

I was suspicious of Richard's sudden good humor. Maybe he was trying to make amends to everyone for being such a jerk earlier today.

"Shall we sit?" Adele made a show of locating her place card and then waited for Richard to pull out her chair. "Jane's chair is right there beside yours, Uncle Dickie. Would you kindly seat her as well?"

"Of course." He pulled my chair away from the table.

I murmured my thanks as I sat.

There could be no doubt that Adele had made the seating arrangements this evening. Mr. Briggs sat at one end of the table with me and Mary to his right and left. Richard was sandwiched between me and Adele, and Father Francis was on Adele's right. Edward was at the other end of the table with Blanche to his right. St. John sat between Blanche and Diana.

"Richard, I'd be happy to switch places with you," St. John said.

"That won't be necessary." Adele glared at him. "Here come our servers. We have no time for musical chairs."

The salvers were brought around, and everyone got down to the business of filling our plates and our bellies. Well, almost everyone.

"Did you know Jane is a wonderful artist?" Adele asked.

"I *do* know—"

"Uncle Dickie—" Adele cut off St. John as if he hadn't spoken. "—would you please sit for Jane to draw your portrait after dinner? I want a likeness of you to put in my room."

"Must we do that today?" I asked.

While I did want an opportunity to talk with Richard Mason alone, I couldn't draw to save my life. What if Richard was the killer, and I disrespected him with an ugly portrait? It'd be curtains for me, that's what—and I'm not talking about those brocade drapes that would look super nice in my living room back home.

"Yes, we must." The child's sharp voice sliced through my thoughts like a knife through cake.

"All right, my sweet," Richard said.

"In the garden after dinner?" she asked.

He and I both nodded.

She smiled and dropped the subject.

I kept my eyes trained on my plate. No way was I going to risk glancing at either St. John or Blanche. "Mmm, what tasty fish."

Ever the trooper, Father Francis said, "Indeed. My compliments to the chef."

Dinner both seemed to drag on forever and be over

much too soon. Contradictory, I know, but the task before me was going to be even more awkward than trying not to make eye contact with the people directly across from me during an entire meal.

Nibbling on a small square of cheese and hoping to make it last for another hour or two, I found my efforts to be in vain when Adele announced that dinner was over and that there was still plenty of light outside for me to draw Uncle Dickie's portrait.

"Yay." I stood. "I'll go get my art supplies."

"I will help you carry them, Jane," Father Francis said.

"Yes, please." If Vidocq stayed in the garden with Richard and me, we might be able to get some pertinent information out of Richard.

"Can you draw?" I whispered, as we entered the schoolroom.

"*Oui.*"

"You can? What a relief."

"I can draw the conclusions." He laughed.

I, on the other hand, couldn't even manage a smile. "I'm screwed here, Vidocq."

"What is the screwed?"

"Jane can draw. I cannot. What am I going to do?"

Placing his chin in his hand for a moment, he said, "Sketch."

"But I can't."

"You can. Do a rough drawing and let no one see it, promising to reveal your masterpiece only when it is finished—which it will never be."

I grinned. "You're a genius."

"*Oui.*"

"Will you stay in the garden with us?" I asked.

"And have the little one cut out my heart? No, thank you. I will come back inside and console Miss Ingram."

"Poor you," I said.

* * *

AFTER HELPING me set up my easel, Father Francis scurried back inside to the salon.

"I'm sorry about this forced labor," Richard said, as he sat on one of the nearby benches. "I know you'd rather be inside with your friends."

"And you'd rather be inside too." I smiled. "A rough sketch won't take long, and it will give me something to work with to complete the final portrait."

"Oh. That doesn't sound so bad then."

"Did you think we'd be out here for hours?" I asked.

"I did." He leaned back against the bench. "Do I need to pose or anything?"

"Relax. I know Adele would prefer a natural-looking portrait." I stretched out my arm, extended my thumb, and squinted. It's something I'd seen artists do on television, so I hoped it would help me seem to know what I was doing. "She adores you. And it's apparent you have a great deal of affection for her as well."

"You think that even after I behaved brutishly toward her earlier today?"

Picking up a piece of charcoal, I said, "I do. Everyone loses his temper on occasion."

"Even you?" he asked.

"Especially me when I was younger. My refusal to keep my mouth closed got me in a lot of trouble when I was a child. How about you?"

"I endured my share of punishments—most of them justly."

I looked at him and then drew an oval on the canvas. "What about Bertha?"

"What about her?" His voice took on an edge.

"I always thought that if I'd had a sibling, we'd get into mischief together." I swirled the charcoal to make two shoulder-like shapes.

"Oh...yes." His voice had softened again. "We did engage in some puckishness now and again."

"You miss her."

"I do."

I drew an eye.

Oh, Reader, that eye was way too big. I wished I could erase it, but I couldn't.

"I wish I could fix it," I mumbled aloud.

"Thank you," he said. "I wasn't aware you..." He sighed. "I didn't know you cared about Bertha."

"I did. I do. I truly would like to have been able to help her."

"No one could." He bowed his head. "We argued before she died. She became convinced I was against her. She believed everyone was against her."

Putting down the charcoal, I went to sit beside him. "She knew you loved her. We all go through that phase sometimes where we feel we're fighting against adversity all on our own, don't we? But deep down, we know we're loved."

"Do we?"

"Absolutely. There's a little girl in the salon who would fight a tiger for you."

He nodded. "There is. I should go inside and give her a hug." Glancing toward the easel, he asked, "Do you need any help with that?"

"No. I've got it." I went back to my canvas and quickly rolled it up before he could see that I'd turned him into a cyclops.

Father Francis intercepted me before I got back to the house. "How did you do on the sketch?"

I showed him.

"*Sacre bleu!* You think Richard Mason is a monster, *non?*"

"Not so much now that I've spoken with him," I said. "I believe he cared deeply for his sister and is grieving her death. And, by his own admission as well as one of the letters I read, he and Bertha argued before she was murdered."

"Ah, but that gives him motive."

"Maybe. But he seemed regretful that they weren't able to make amends."

"Never forget, *ma petite*, everyone shows you what he wants you to see."

"True." I figured I'd better talk quickly because I didn't know how much time we'd have undisturbed.

"Another letter I read was from Bertha's sister. She was dying and was expressing her appreciation to Bertha for taking in her child—Adele. In the novel, Adele was the daughter of Edward's French mistress. How can her history be so far removed from what it was originally? I wasn't even aware Bertha had a sister."

"This is due to the destruction of the silverfish. Whatever they have ruined affects the events of the book going forward, be that personalities, histories, or events."

"Does Richard know Adele is his niece?" I asked. "He didn't let on to me if he does."

Shrugging, he said, "I imagine we shall soon see."

"What did you discover from the letters you read?"

"The same as you. Bertha was feuding with her brother. Taking the matter even farther, she was corresponding with Mr. Briggs to rewrite her will. She wanted Richard out and intended to leave everything to Adele."

"Were you able to determine if the will was changed before Bertha died?"

"*Non*, I was not."

"I'll see if Edward knows or if Mr. Briggs will tell me. Thank you."

"You are most welcome."

"And what are we thanking the gracious Father Francis for?" St. John asked as he came out of the house.

Vidocq opened his mouth to answer, but I beat him to the punch. "Father Francis has agreed to perform our marriage ceremony next month." I guessed we'd have either solved the murders of Bertha and Grace or died ourselves by then. Either way, the delay tactic had worked with the drawing, and I was eager to use it again.

"But why must we wait?" St. John asked.

"He has been called away and must leave tomorrow," I said. "But he'll be back soon."

St. John looked at Father Francis. "Will you be gone an entire month?"

"It is hard to say." Father Francis smiled at me. He knew well what I was doing.

"I was hoping we'd be in India before this month was out," St. John said.

"India will still be there and will need us every bit as badly in a month," I said. "We have only one opportunity for our marriage ceremony to be performed by the man I consider my godfather."

St. John opened his mouth to speak but then closed it again. That was the smartest thing I'd seen him do yet.

"Are you sure you require no assistance with this?" Father Francis asked.

"Actually, this easel is a bit awkward to carry." I handed it to him. "I appreciate your chivalry."

"I am happy to be of service."

"I can take it for you," St. John said.

"That's okay." I smiled. "We'll see you in the salon in a few moments…dear."

As Vidocq and I dropped off the art supplies, he said, "I almost hate leaving you alone here with St. John."

I scoffed. "Don't worry. I can handle him."

"*Oui*, but can he handle you?"

Mr. Briggs stopped us in the hallway on our way to the salon. "Excuse me, Father Francis, but may I have a private word with Miss Eyre?"

"Of course." He gave me a nod before walking ever so slowly in the direction of the salon.

"Did you ever locate Mrs. Rochester's diary?" Briggs asked.

"No, but I believe I have something even better—her correspondence. I understand that at one point, she was considering cutting Richard out of her will and leaving everything to Adele. Did she, in fact, make those changes?"

"Nothing had been finalized, and her original last will and testament stood as of the date of her death." He looked around before leaning in closer. "What else did you discover?"

"I found out Adele is actually Bertha Rochester's niece." I drew my brows together. "Isn't it odd she and Mr. Rochester would prefer to pretend Adele was simply their ward rather than a member of the family?"

"You must remember, Mrs. Rochester was a madwoman. Not everything she said was true."

"Then Adele wasn't her niece?" I asked.

"Well, that particular piece of information was accurate. I'm merely pointing out that you shouldn't rely on everything you read without verification. For example, Mrs. Rochester detested her brother one day and loved him the next. That's why I never changed her original will."

"But if Richard thought his sister was considering cutting him out of her will, might that have given him the incentive to kill her before she could?"

"Yes, but once again, it's wise to not be hasty," he said. "Where are the letters now? May I have them?"

"I have put them in a safe place and will give them to you tomorrow."

"All right. Please use discretion."

"Always," I said.

EDWARD KNOCKED from inside my wardrobe soon after everyone had gone to bed. Not willing to take any chances, I asked, "Is it you?"

"Of course. Would a murderer have knocked?"

"Probably not." I opened the door. "Please tell me how I can secure this contraption. It has worried me ever since I found out about it."

"It's really quite simple." He shoved the wardrobe down far enough to block the door leading into the hallway and also block the door into the wardrobe.

"Wow. Why didn't I think of that?"

"I'm sure you would have, especially if I hadn't led you to believe it was difficult." He spread his hands. "What can I say? I wanted the opportunity to talk with you alone."

"I've been wanting that too." I pushed the dresser in front of the bedchamber door.

"Are you trying to keep me from getting out?" he teased.

"You're free to go anytime, but I'm rather paranoid about who else might try to get in."

"Fair enough." He walked over to the bed. "May I sit?"

"Sure."

He sat at the head of the bed, and I perched at the foot on the other side and faced him.

"How's Cooper?" he asked.

"He's well. I wish he'd have prepared me better for this—" I had no idea what to call the situation in which I'd found myself, so I let it go at "this."

"Don't be too tough on him. If he'd told you what you were in for, would you have believed him?"

"No. I'd have thought he was insane."

"Most people can't comprehend another world beyond what they know."

"True," I said. "When I first opened my reticule, I found a note from Cooper. We had an entire conversation, and then he burned the paper on his side of the portal—or whatever you call where he is with regard to where we are."

"Portal will do." A smile played about the corners of his mouth. "I came up with that method of communication. That system has served us well. It's how I knew you were coming here."

"If I put a note into the reticule, will he get it?"

"He will. Whether he'll answer it or not depends on his assessment of the situation." He leaned forward and took my hand. "If you're going to be a proper archivist, you need to learn how to navigate Literatia on your own. He'll always be around to help, but—"

"How?" I interrupted. "I asked him to join me in this rescue mission since it was my first, but he said he couldn't."

"And yet he sent the private detective Vidocq to assist you."

"Cooper didn't send me Vidocq. I found him on my own."

"He wouldn't have been in town had the publisher not received a warning that Vidocq might be considering taking his memoir elsewhere." He chuckled. "Trust me. I know Cooper. He's doing all he can to ensure this mission is a success."

"But it's my understanding he can't keep us from failing."

"That's true. He has given us the tools we need. It's up to us to make the most of them."

I blew out a breath. "Despite the tools, there's still no guarantee though."

He raised my hand to his lips and kissed it. "Where would the fun and excitement be in knowing the end even before we knew the beginning?" He released my hand. "Come up here."

I hesitated.

"No ulterior motive, I promise," he said.

Standing, I moved to the head of the bed and sat beside him.

He put his arm around me. "Rest your head on my shoulder, and let's discuss and strategize."

"Discuss and strategize—I like that." I placed my head on his shoulder. It felt nice—it felt right. "You smell good."

"Thanks. I took a bath today. Brushed my teeth too."

I laughed softly. "I've got a feeling I'll never live that down. Once again, I feel there are some things Cooper could have prepared me for a little better—like the silverfish."

"No need to have you overly concerned about them right off the bat. Now tell me, what have you learned so far?"

I told him about St. John's visits to cure Bertha of her madness, about the letters, about the rift between Richard and Bertha, and about Adele. "Were you aware Adele is Bertha's niece?"

"Richard's child?" he asked.

"No. Bertha had a sister. I should've asked Richard about her when we were in the garden, but there didn't seem to be a good way to broach the subject.

"Adele's parentage has deviated much from the original narrative. The silverfish have already destroyed a great deal of the novel. We're running out of time."

"I thought the silverfishes' goal was to kill Edward Rochester," I said.

"It is, but if they can undermine the integrity of the book well enough, they can demolish it without removing a main character. May I see those letters?"

"Vidocq has some of them, but I'll give you the ones I started reading through." I got up and retrieved the letters from beneath the mattress.

"Thanks. I'll read them before I go to sleep."

I sat back down on the bed.

"In case I forgot to mention it, I'm grateful for everything you're doing to help me," he said.

My head fell back against the pillows as my eyelids began to droop.

"Poor Gia. You're exhausted."

Lips curving into a smile, I said, "I like hearing you call me by my real name."

"I know. Come and push this wardrobe slightly aside after I leave, and then you can go to sleep."

"All right."

He took my hand and led me over to the wardrobe. Before moving the heavy piece of furniture, he kissed my forehead. "Goodnight, Gia." He moved the wardrobe, just enough to slip out the door into the passageway. Then he waited to make sure I was able to move it back far enough to bar the entrance before he left me.

I was looking forward to getting to know him better once we were back home in North Carolina. Surely if *he* had a crazy wife in an attic somewhere, he'd have told me —right?

CHAPTER 18

As tired as I was, I became fully awake a couple of hours later when I heard my doorknob turning. Sitting up in the bed, I pulled the covers to my chin and listened intently.

Who was out there? Was it a person? Someone strong enough to open the door, despite the dresser blocking the way? Was it a silverfish? If it *was* a silverfish, it could theoretically disassemble itself, slither under the door, and then reassemble—couldn't it? While I'd have loved to know exactly what it was that I might end up having to fight, I didn't want to call out and let the thing know I was awake.

Easing out of bed, I gingerly placed my feet on the floor. Nothing squished between my toes or crawled up my leg. That was a relief.

I managed to make it to the dresser and light a candle. Directing the flame like a very weak flashlight beam, I scanned the floor and then looked around for a weapon. The room was void of silverfish—yay—but also of weapons—boo.

I went to stand by the dressing table. If necessary, I could use the legs of the stool to crush silverfish as they came under the door, or I could hit a person with the stool and try to escape out the door.

The doorknob rattling abruptly stopped as I was constructing my defense, and I heard the footsteps of whatever had been outside the door retreating down the hall. I remained by the dressing table for a full minute before allowing myself to believe my would-be intruder wasn't coming back.

Although my heart was pounding so rapidly and heavily that it almost hurt, I was desperate to know what enemy would've planned to attack me while I slept. I shoved aside the dresser, picked my candlestick back up, and slowly opened the door.

There was a dark figure—it appeared to be a man—creeping down the hallway. Leaving my door ajar, I tiptoed toward the figure. Hopefully, I could get close enough to get a better idea of who—or what—it was. After all, it could be one of the silverfish creatures. But truth be told, I'd much prefer to discover I was following a human.

When the figure turned to enter a room, I saw his profile.

"St. John!"

He whirled around. "Jane. What are you doing?"

"What are *you* doing? Are you going to deny it was you who was trying to get into my room?"

"No, I don't deny that. I just—" His eyes dropped to the floor as he started walking toward me. "I wanted to make sure you were all right."

"Baloney!"

He brought his eyes back up to mine. "Ba—balooney?"

"Baloney," I repeated, realizing baloney probably hadn't been invented yet. "It's a French word Father Francis taught me. It means *nonsense*. Now what were you really doing? Were you going to take advantage of me?"

"No. I—" He frowned. "I wanted to make sure no one else was."

I gasped. "How dare you? If that's the way you feel about me, why—" I broke off. "Do you smell that? It's smoke."

Forget, St. John! Reader, the house was on fire!

"Fire!" I yelled, as I ran down the hall banging my palm on the doors. "The house is on fire!"

St. John called after me, but I ignored him. He needed to either help or get out of the way.

Diana flung open her door. "What's happening?"

"There's a fire," I said. "Smell the smoke?"

"I do." She started knocking on doors on the other side of the hall.

Father Francis and Mary came to see how they could help. Okay, more accurately, Father Francis was helping.

Mary was sprinting toward the stairs to make her way out of the burning building.

Way to think of others, Mary.

I slapped on a door, and it opened. "Edward!"

His bed was in flames, and he was trying to beat them out with a blanket.

"Get out! I don't want you getting hurt!"

Heck with that. I jerked a pair of curtains down and began using one of the panels to smother the flames. Father Francis took the other panel and aided in tamping down the fire.

Diana ran out of the room but came back momentarily with blankets. She shoved one at St. John and began beating the sparks on the floor near the bed with the other.

From somewhere behind us, I heard Briggs exclaim, "What in blazes," which was—probably inadvertently— spot on. He, too, procured a blanket from somewhere, and before long, we had extinguished the fire.

"Thank you, everyone." Edward looked at me. "Are we all unharmed?"

We smelled like a barbecue pit and were coughing pretty badly, but none of us was too worse for wear.

The same event had occurred in the original novel— Edward's bed had been ignited as he slept. Bertha was the arsonist then. I scrutinized the faces surrounding me and wondered who'd lit the fire tonight. Had St. John not tried to get into my room, Edward might've had to fight the fire on his own. Why hadn't Edward raised the alarm himself? I had so many unanswered questions.

"Let's go down and get some brandy," Edward said. "It'll help calm our nerves."

"Where will you sleep now?" I asked.

"This is Thornfield, Miss Eyre. If there's anything we have an abundance of, it's guestrooms."

Edward's sleeping arrangements were actually the least of my concerns. I only hoped we'd get time to address them before another attempt was made on his life. That private conversation wasn't likely to take place tonight, however—or until later that day, if you prefer— because seven of us were sitting in the salon in our smoky-smelling nightclothes sipping brandy.

"What on earth happened?" Mary asked, as if she really gave a hoot and had stayed to help the rest of us extinguish the fire. Her nightdress was the only exception to the smoky aroma rule. "Did you knock over your candle?"

Her question made me feel defensive on Edward's behalf. I knew, based on my knowledge of the original manuscript, that the fire in his room was set intentionally.

Edward took the high road. "I suppose I must have. I was reading and dozed off."

My questioning eyes sought his. *The letters.*

He gave me a slight nod to indicate yes, they had burned.

Even though we knew what we knew, we couldn't use

the letters as actual evidence now. Both he and I could testify as to what we'd read, but the judge would likely see our testimony as a collusive effort to free Edward at best and to frame someone else at worst. But the letters in Vidocq's possession were still okay.

"I wonder why neither Mr. Mason, Miss Ingram, nor any of the servants reacted to our calls for help," Diana said.

"They're in another wing," Briggs said. "Had we been unable to extinguish the blaze on our own, I'd have run to the kitchen and sounded the gong."

Based on Briggs' response, I could assume Richard, Blanche, and Adele—along with the servants and the silverfish—had snoozed peacefully through this pre-dawn adventure, leading me to the conclusion that our arsonist was here in the room with us. While it was entirely possible any one of them would have time to sneak into Edward's room, set the fire, and scurry back to his or her bed, my suspicions currently landed squarely on St. John.

I looked over to see that he was staring down into his glass of brandy. What was he thinking? Was he feeling guilty for his actions? Was he angry that his plan to kill Edward had failed? Or was he innocent and fearful that I might tell everyone he'd been skulking around outside my door shortly before we discovered the fire?

Having one last sip of my brandy, I got up and placed the glass on the sideboard. "I'm going back upstairs to bed. I'll see you all at breakfast."

For once, St. John didn't offer to escort me, but Mary and Diana also rose and accompanied me up the stairs.

"Thank you for speaking with St. John on my behalf," Mary said softly. "He has given me his blessing to marry whomever I choose."

"I'm glad," I said. "Congratulations."

"I only hope we'll be as happy as the two of you."

If you only knew, sister... "I hope you'll be even happier."

OVER BREAKFAST THAT MORNING, everyone was in a dither over the fire, especially those who'd been absent during the excitement of it all.

"Uncle Dickie, please take me away from here at once," Adele said, folding her bony arms across her chest. "Thornfield Hall is cursed, and we're all doomed to die if we stay here."

"Adele, darling, don't you think you're overreacting?" Blanche asked.

If Blanche thought Adele had been overreacting before, she would undoubtedly think the tween's next performance worthy of the Royal Shakespeare Company.

"You don't understand anything!" Adele burst into tears. "You don't even care. You wish I *would* die so you could have Uncle Dickie all to yourself. Well, you can't have him! He likes Jane now, and we're all leaving here together—today." She knocked over her chair in her haste to get away from the table and fled the room.

Most of us realized that outburst was simply the ranting of a scared, angry child. Most of us.

I said to Richard, "Shall I go up and see about her?"

"I'll do it," he said. "Eat your breakfast, and I'll try to cajole her into coming back and finishing hers." He grinned. "After all, the house wouldn't be so cruel as to kill us all before we've finished this lovely meal, would it?"

"Let's hope not," I replied with a smile.

Before I'd taken my next bite of food, St. John threw his napkin onto the table. "What's this about the three of you leaving here together?"

Richard stopped, but I told him to go ahead and check on Adele. Then I turned my attention to St. John and took Adele's place on the proverbial theater company stage.

"Are you stupid?" I asked. "I mean, seriously, I'd believed you to be an intelligent man. Yet here you are letting your mind be swayed by a child. Do you also think the house is cursed? If so, you should pack up and leave it. Just know I won't be going with you."

Instead of focusing on me, St. John let his stunned gaze take in all the other faces at the table, as if they were all aware that I was behaving hysterically. "Jane, please—"

"No." I cut off whatever patronizing thing he was about to say. "I'm through with your garbage. Last night, you came to my room and scared me half out of my wits."

"What?" Diana placed her hand on her chest. "St. John, what were you *thinking?*"

"I believe it's apparent he doesn't trust me to be a virtuous woman. Still, it's a good thing I investigated my middle-of-the-night visitor or else we might not have known about the fire in Mr. Rochester's room until it had gotten out of hand."

"Jane, wouldn't it be more seemly for us to have this conversation in private?" St. John asked.

"It would have been before you further insulted me by questioning whether I planned to leave Thornfield Hall with Mr. Mason and Adele." I stood. "Now we have nothing further to discuss either publicly or privately." Grabbing the scone that I hadn't had a chance to eat, I left the room. Or, to put it in theater vernacular, I exited stage right.

CHAPTER 19

Father Francis followed me out into the garden where I sat on a bench eating my scone.

"Were you sent to placate *this* child?" I asked.

He chuckled. "What child? I see only a fiery young *mademoiselle* who gave an insolent gentleman the tongue-lashing he deserved."

I held out the scone. "Want some?"

"*Non, merci.* I ate my breakfast while watching the performances. Tell me more about this encounter with St. John. He attempted to get into your bedchamber?"

"Yes. I was terrified when I heard someone rattling the knob, but the urge to know who'd tried to come in while I slept overtook my common sense, so I opened the door and went into the hallway to see who was there."

"When you speak with him alone, ask Edward what he thinks actually caused the fire," he said. "Edward does not strike me as the type to be careless."

"Me either. In the novel, Edward's bed was set on fire by Bertha. Since St. John was awake and wandering the halls, it makes me wonder if he set the fire. But if he'd already been in Edward's room and knew he wasn't in mine—which is what he intimated to me that he thought—then why would he come to my room?"

"Perhaps for the same reason any man would go to a woman's room." He waggled his bushy eyebrows. "He thought perhaps that as Edward was burning in *his* bed, it could be that you were burning in yours with the love for him."

I felt my face flush, and Vidocq laughed.

"I am sorry for embarrassing you," he said. "On a serious note, I do not know if St. John killed Bertha and Grace or set fire to Edward's bed, but I'm convinced he is a danger to you. Continue to be on your greatest guard against him."

"You think he wants to harm me?"

"He wants to possess you, *ma petite*, and he will do whatever it takes to achieve his aim."

With sudden clarity, I asked, "What would happen if St. John kidnapped me? Would it damage the novel?"

"Not only that, but the curator who delivered you to Literatia might not be able to retrieve you."

I gulped. "I won't let myself be alone with him again."

"That's very wise." He opened his arms. "Now, give Father Francis the hug before I leave."

Stepping into his embrace, I said, "I feel we've been friends forever. I don't want you to go."

"I will return if I am needed," he said. "And, if not, I will see you again—in another book or in another place. Stay watchful."

"You too." Tears burned my eyes as I kissed his cheek. "You really are the best detective ever, you know."

"*Oui. A bientot.* See you soon."

"Father Francis!" It was Edward calling as he strode down the garden path. "I'm glad I caught you. Thank you again for your help."

The two men shook hands.

"Protect her," Vidocq said.

Edward nodded. "I will."

And then Vidocq walked away.

I wiped the tears from my eyes, and Edward gave me a quick one-armed squeeze, knowing we had to be mindful of prying eyes.

"Let's walk," I said.

As we strolled farther away from the house, I asked him to tell me the truth about the fire.

"I did fall asleep while reading the letters," he said. "Being in a comfortable bed again was a powerful sedative. But, no, I didn't knock over a candle as Mary suggested."

"I never believed you did. Do you think St. John might've set your bed on fire before coming to my room?"

He shrugged. "It's possible."

"Why didn't you have your doors locked and barred? You knew you were in more danger than I was."

"That knowledge was precisely why I left my bedchamber open to attack. Underestimating my fatigue, I thought I'd awaken the moment anyone entered the room. Then I'd force the miscreant to give me the truth."

"And force him or her to confess to the judge." I sighed. "Promise me you won't take a risk like that again. You could've been seriously hurt."

Smiling slightly, he said, "I feel your concern goes beyond your need to free me so you can go home."

Warmth rushed to my face. "I wouldn't want to see anyone get hurt."

"Anyone? That's a strong protest from the woman who roasted St. John Rivers alive at the breakfast table in front of kith and kin."

"Where I come from, we'd say 'in front of God and everybody.'" I paused. "Do you think I owe him an apology?"

"Do you?"

"No. I mean, I guess I could've aired my grievances more maturely and in private." I picked a daisy and twirled it between my thumb and forefinger. "I was really scared when he tried to open my door last night. I thought someone was coming to kill me—and he very well might have been."

"I rather doubt it," he said.

"Even if we give him the benefit of believing he didn't come to my room with murder on his mind, wouldn't a normal man have let me know he planned to visit me in the middle of the night?"

Edward stopped walking. "Was not knowing who was there the only deterrent to your opening the door?"

"You know it wasn't. Had he told me he planned a visit in the wee hours of the morning, I'd have told him to stay in his own room and not disturb me. On the other hand, you told me you were coming, and I welcomed you right into the room."

"You did indeed. Does that mean I can come back tonight?"

Reader, I simply stared at him with my mouth hanging open.

"F-for what p-purpose?" I managed to stutter at last.

He threw back his head and laughed. "I owe Cooper a huge debt of gratitude."

"Why? He hasn't gotten us out of here yet."

"No, but he sent me you. What a breath of fresh air you are."

Flustered, I resumed walking. "Any ideas about what we should do next?"

"I'm not sure. Does that invitation to your room still stand?"

I turned and thew my flower at him. It fell to the ground in front of him, and he bent and picked it up.

Smiling, he said, "You are indeed a treasure."

EDWARD SUGGESTED we go back inside separately. When I went through the door, Diana was waiting for me in the foyer.

"I know St. John behaved abominably, but won't you please speak with him?" she asked.

"Only if you'll stay with us."

"All right. He's in the library."

I followed her down the hall and into the room. St. John stood by the window, the sunlight at his back.

"Jane." He crossed the room to take both my hands. "Thank you, Diana. Could you please leave us now?"

"I've asked her not to," I said. "I'm very hurt by your actions, St. John. What have I done to make you so distrustful of me?"

St. John glanced at Diana.

"Anything you have to say to me, I feel certain you can say in front of Diana. Your sister adores you and wants the best for you." As an afterthought, I added, "As do I." I *did* want what was best for him as long as that "best" had nothing to do with me.

Sighing, he ran a hand over his face. "It was Bertha. She told me the first time I visited her that Adele's governess was a woman of easy virtue intent on destroying her marriage."

"That's absurd," Diana said. "She must have been talking about some other governess."

"Exactly." I didn't know anything about the version of Jane Eyre I was currently impersonating, so Bertha might have been spot on. Still....

"Keep in mind this conversation with Bertha took place before I ever met you, Jane, so it didn't occur to me to question the woman's assertion." St. John paced. "Then I found you, and I became so enamored of you that I didn't even remember what Bertha had said until the evening I returned you here to Thornfield Hall."

"The night Bertha died," I said.

"Right," he said. "And I saw how pleased Edward was that you'd returned—"

"You've met Adele," I interrupted. "Why *wouldn't* the man be pleased? Do you honestly think Mr. Rochester is capable of handling her on his own?"

"Capable, yes," Diana said. "Willing, maybe not. Either way, I feel Jane's point is valid—the man would have been delighted to have Adele's governess returned."

"Even so, it appeared to me that he was smitten with Jane." He returned to the window. "And I feared the feeling was mutual."

"But were you misjudging a friendship based on the words of—" I shrugged.

"A madwoman?" Diana finished for me.

"Possibly. I was planning to speak with Bertha the next day—ask her for specifics, make sure it was *you* she'd been referencing in our previous conversation." He resumed pacing. "She died before I could visit her."

"Then why didn't you question me?" I placed a hand on his arm, so he'd stand still for a moment. "You said you wanted to marry me. Why would you even consider spending the rest of your life with a woman you couldn't trust?"

"I kept telling myself that when we got to India, everything would be different. You'd forget about the Rochesters and Thornfield Hall—even Adele—because you'd have me and our work and, later, our children."

Reader, I felt sorry for St. John then—but only a little. It was still possible he was a murderer.

"What do you say, Jane, dear?" Diana asked. "As Shakespeare said in *Othello*, 'he loves not wisely but too well.' Will you forgive my brother?"

"I do forgive St. John." I dropped my hand from his arm. "But I can't commit to marriage with a man who questions my fidelity."

CHAPTER 20

After leaving the library on the heels of St. John's declaration that he'd do whatever it took to win me back, I made my way to the dining room where I'd spotted a large bowl of capped strawberries earlier. The scone I'd grabbed when I'd left the breakfast table hadn't taken the edge off my hunger, and I hoped the berries were still there. I didn't want to go scrounge around in the kitchen, especially if Silverfish Fairfax was there.

Success! The berries were on the sideboard. I was stuffing one into my mouth when Richard Mason strolled into the room.

"I'd heard you also abandoned breakfast in a huff," he said with a slight smile.

"I did. And now you'll have no doubt whatsoever that I'm a bad influence on Adele." I held out the bowl. "Want some?"

He took a berry. "It could alternatively be said that *she's* the troublesome influence."

"Hardly. I was inciting chaos long before Adele was born." I ate another of the delicious berries. "How is she, by the way?"

"Fine. It didn't take me long to calm her down. Blanche, on the other hand, is proving more difficult to appease."

"Forgive my saying so, but I hope Miss Ingram can understand the upheaval Adele is going through. Despite Adele's saying she doesn't care about what happens to Mr. Rochester, the child has to be traumatized by everything that's been taking place in this house. You're the only steady person in her life."

"I wouldn't say that. She admires you more than you know, Miss Eyre."

"I have a confession—I know Adele is your niece." I met his gaze squarely to gauge his reaction to my statement.

His face softened. "Did Bertha tell you?"

"No. Your other sister had written Mrs. Rochester a letter. Father Francis discovered it in Grace's room and brought it to me. We both understood the need to be discreet, as Adele's relationship to the Mason family isn't common knowledge." I paused. "Does *she* know?"

"No. Briggs has been instructed not to divulge the information to her until my guardianship has been secured."

"How does the fact that Mr. Rochester might be exonerated affect your petition?"

Eyes darkening, he said, "I'm aware you believe in Edward's innocence. Perhaps Bertha was right, and you're in love with him. Perhaps you can't imagine Edward slashing a knife across my sister's throat as she slept. Or perhaps you simply want to believe the best of everyone. But you are sorely mistaken in your assessment of Edward's character."

He stalked off, leaving me feeling like we were back on unfriendly terms. Although, I guess it was unlikely that we ever were on *friendly* terms. He tolerated me for Adele's sake, and I pumped him for information to determine if he'd murdered his sister for financial gain. So, not a great foundation for b-f-fs.

No longer hungry, I placed the bowl of strawberries back where I'd found them. As I left the dining room, it struck me that Richard Mason wouldn't kill Bertha for profit or out of anger, but he might choose to end her suffering. The man obviously believed Edward to be a monster for keeping Bertha locked in her attic room. And while that was admittedly cruel, I knew the insane asylums of this era were reputed to be atrocious. Of course, I couldn't speak for Bertha, but if I'd had been given a choice between Thornfield Hall and an asylum, I'd have taken Thornfield Hall hands down.

I had no idea how Jane—either the original or the Literatia version—felt about Bertha's plight, but my heart ached for the woman. Resigning myself to the fact that I could do nothing to help Bertha in any version of *Jane Eyre*, I went in search of Edward.

In his study, I found Mr. Briggs alone. He was sitting at the desk. Having taken off his jacket and rolled up his shirtsleeves, he'd also opened the window. A breeze was gently ruffling the drapes.

"Hello, Mr. Briggs. I was looking for Mr. Rochester."

"I do believe he's resting at the moment. Is there anything I may help you with?"

Shaking my head, I said, "I simply wanted to make sure he wasn't the worse for wear after last night's fire." I took a seat in front of the desk. "I'm awfully sorry some of Mrs. Rochester's letters burned up in the fire. They could have been useful to Mr. Rochester's defense."

"Some? I was under the impression that they were all destroyed."

"Thankfully, Father Francis was in possession of a few of them. So all is not lost."

"Where are those letters now?" he asked. "Do you have them?"

"I don't. Father Francis didn't mention them before he left this morning, and I forgot to ask him about them." My lips curved into a faint smile as the wind brought the scent of lavender into the room. "That smells delightful. I wonder if I opened my bedchamber window the scent of lavender would fill the room?"

"Miss Eyre, it's imperative that we find those letters

immediately. Do you have any idea where they could be?"

"I can go take a look in the room where Father Francis slept."

He stood. "Do that. Do it at once please."

I noticed his waistcoat was missing a button. Rising from the chair, I fished the button from my pocket. "Is this yours?"

"Yes, thank you." He took the button. "Would you see to those letters now? We haven't got time to waste."

"Of course."

Mr. Briggs had snagged the button from my hand without a second thought. He hadn't asked where I'd found it or why I'd been carrying it around with me. Was he so nonchalant about the button because he had nothing to hide? It was possible he'd lost it in Bertha Rochester's room while they were discussing her will. Or had he lost it when he was there for a more carnal purpose, and he simply thought it unlikely that I'd guess him to have been her lover?

I WENT to the room Vidocq had so recently vacated, but he'd either left nothing behind or the maid who'd cleaned the room had taken the letters. The maid hadn't finished working here because the bed had been stripped and was in the process of being remade.

I moved over to the window while I waited for the

maid to return. I could see Richard and Adele walking on the lawn. Hopefully, he was telling her of their kinship.

I found it horribly sad that Bertha hadn't claimed Adele as her niece and treated her as a treasured member of the family all along. Had Bertha not allowed herself to get close to Adele because she was frightened her violent tendencies would be uncontrollable around the child? Or was the issue irrelevant since Adele wasn't Bertha's niece until the silverfish damaged the book? Before I could ruminate on the current plotline any further, the maid returned and pulled me back into what was passing as my real world these days.

"I didn't expect anyone to be here," she said, hesitating in the doorway with an armful of clean linens. "I can come back."

"No, please don't let me interrupt your work. I was waiting for you to make sure Father Francis hadn't left a packet of letters behind."

"I didn't see anything lying about, miss," she said. "Shall I go through the dresser?"

"I'll do it. You go ahead and make the bed. I don't want to keep you from your duties."

Doubtful Vidocq would be so careless or forgetful as to leave Bertha's letters in the dresser, I still checked every drawer. They were empty.

After thanking the maid, I resumed my search for Edward. Briggs had said he was resting. I supposed the room Edward now occupied was near the one that had been on fire, so that room was where I began.

I went inside the scorched room. The windows were bare since I'd ripped down the curtains to help fight the fire, and the sun streamed in to illuminate the charred bed.

The room itself didn't appear to have suffered a great deal of damage. The bed, the drapes, and the rug by the bed were a complete loss, but those things shouldn't be difficult to replace; and I couldn't see any structural damage. I opened the window to help dispel the smell of smoke.

I glanced at the bed again and shivered. Edward had been lucky.

"What are you doing?"

I whirled around to see Edward leaning against the door jamb with his hands in his pockets.

"I'm looking for you," I said.

"Did you think I'd flown out the window?"

"I...he...Mr. Briggs—" Why did this man make me so flustered?

He laughed softly and came into the room. "You have found me."

"Yes. I happened to remember that Vidocq had some of Bertha's letters. I forgot to ask him to return them to me, and they weren't in his room. Any chance he gave them to you?"

"He did indeed. I've been reading them, and one in particular is quite eye-opening." He jerked his head toward the door. "Shall we?"

"Sure. Do you think this eye-opener will buy you your freedom?"

"It very well could."

I followed him down the hall and into his temporary room. He closed the door, walked over to the bed, and took the letter from beneath the mattress. Sitting on the bed, he patted the space beside him.

I sat next to him and watched as he unfolded the letter. "I'm confused about why Vidocq wouldn't have mentioned this letter to me if it contains something relevant. Do you think he read it?"

"Oh, he read it—that's why he spoke to me about it rather than you. In the letter, Bertha's sister is asking Bertha about her lover, who she refers to as *R*. I imagine they used that initial so that if she was ever asked about it, Bertha could say they were talking about Edward."

"How can you be certain they weren't?" I asked. "You're no more Edward than I am Jane. Maybe the Literatia versions of Edward and Bertha had a passionate relationship."

"Impossible. There's every evidence to support the fact that Edward and Bertha despised each other in both versions of the book," he said. "As far as I've been able to tell, the only difference is that everyone in this iteration knew about Bertha and the fact that she was Edward's wife."

"Did you have any interaction with Bertha? Or were you sent here only after she was murdered?"

"I was sent here while Jane was at Gateshead, but I

didn't have any association with Bertha. At that time, I didn't realize what the silverfish were planning to use to destroy the book. Had I known it would be the woman's murder—and me in the role of villain—I'd have done my due diligence."

"Do you have any idea who stabbed her?"

He held up the letter. "I have a better idea now."

The letter said, in part: "You need to be more careful with *R*. What if you should become pregnant? That would be your downfall. Believe me. I speak from experience. Is his love worth the risk? Are you sure he even loves you at all?"

"Had her sister been speaking of Edward, getting pregnant wouldn't have been a downfall," I said. "Even if Bertha hadn't wanted a baby, her sister would have worded it differently—a risk, maybe—especially if there was a medical reason for avoiding pregnancy." I frowned. "The only other *R* in the house that night was Richard. Surely, *they* weren't—"

"There was Mr. Rivers, remember. He could be *R*. And Briggs' first name is Robert."

"Robert?" I gasped. "How do you know? I don't remember Mr. Briggs' name being revealed in the original."

"It wasn't. I saw his name on my trial documents."

"Then Briggs could certainly be *R*," I said.

"True, but you told me St. John was visiting Bertha in her room, and he didn't deny that."

"But if he'd been having an affair with her, wouldn't he have lied and told me Grace was with them during his visits or something?"

"Not necessarily—unless he did kill Bertha and then murdered Grace to be sure his secret would be kept."

I frowned. "I asked him straight up if he'd been having an affair with Bertha, and he said no."

Arching a brow, he asked, "You expected him to brag about his previous conquests?"

"Not brag, but I held the door wide open to the truth by telling him I understood he had a life before we met and that I wouldn't fault him for prior indiscretions."

Edward said nothing—he merely smiled at me.

I felt compelled to further explain myself. "Oh, come on. I've read enough historical romance novels to know that Victorian men were expected to do anything they wanted while their wives were expected to be as pure as the new fallen snow—or, at least, they had to *appear* to be."

He leaned over and kissed me.

I blinked. "What was that for?"

"I'm savoring the moment, that's all. You taste like strawberries."

"Is that a good thing?"

"Absolutely."

Emboldened by the fact that I was not Jane Eyre but a modern woman who could do as I pleased, I took Edward's face in my hands and kissed him deeply. As the passion flared between us, there was a knock at the door.

Edward pressed the letter into my hand. "Take this and hide in the wardrobe," he whispered. "Stay hidden until I let you know it's safe to come out."

Nodding, I hurried to the wardrobe and climbed inside. Edward pushed the door closed before calling for his visitor to come inside.

It was Briggs. "You look as if you've gotten some rest, my friend. There's a bit of color back in your cheeks."

Reader, I took credit for that heightened color, thank-you-very-much.

"I feel better than I have in quite a while," Edward said.

"I imagine so. One hour's rest in a comfortable bed beats a full night's sleep on a prison cot—only try not to light this bed on fire."

Edward chuckled. "Is that why you came to check on me?"

"Actually, I was upstairs looking for Miss Eyre. She came up a few minutes ago to search for something she thought Father Francis left behind."

"Really? Does she think he found something that could exonerate me?"

"I'm afraid not," Briggs said. "Miss Eyre had mentioned some letters Grace Poole had been holding for your wife. I believe Father Francis might have been snooping in Miss Poole's room and found them after her death, but there was nothing of value to us in them."

That's when I began to feel fingers of ice closing around my throat, Reader. Had he truly believed the letters were of no conse-quence, he wouldn't have been so insistent on my finding them.

"How do you know? Have you read them?"

"I've seen some of Mrs. Rochester's correspondence in the past, and it was completely innocuous. My guess is that Father Francis took the letters and anything else he might have thought valuable when he left Thornfield Hall. I found him to be rather odd."

"I imagine you're right," Edward said.

Part of me wanted to fling open the wardrobe door and defend Vidocq, but I knew to be still—I'd learned that much from Vidocq's memoir.

"Did Miss Eyre mention any such letters to you? Had she read them?" Briggs asked.

"I know nothing about them."

"Ah, good. I'm glad neither she nor Father Francis bothered you with them. I was half afraid he might try to blackmail you, pretending there was something of interest to you in the letters." Briggs tsked. "I hope we've seen the last of him. Are you coming downstairs now?"

"Soon. I'm going to rest for a few minutes more."

"I'll leave you to it."

I heard the door close. Moments later, Edward opened the door to the wardrobe. Stepping into his arms, I hadn't realized I was trembling until he held me tightly.

"It's him." I buried my face in Edward's chest. "I thought maybe he'd lost his waistcoat button in Bertha's room while drafting her will or something. But it's him. He killed her—and Grace. And I think I might be next because he knows that I know."

EDWARD AND I CONCOCTED A PLAN; and while Edward was taking care of his part of the plan, I watched the clock so that I could do my part. Half an hour after Edward had left me at my door, I went downstairs to find Briggs. Luckily, he was still in Edward's study, and he was alone. The plan might still have worked otherwise, but it would have been more difficult.

I went into the study and shut the door almost all the way behind me. Hopefully, he didn't see the way my hands were shaking. "I need to speak with you privately, Mr. Briggs."

"Did you find the letters you'd given to Father Francis?" he asked, barely looking up from the book he was reading.

"I did. That's how I know you were having an affair with Bertha Rochester."

Now I had his attention.

He put down the book and stood. "That's preposterous. Why would you say such a thing?"

"It was plainly written in one of Bertha's letters."

Scoffing, he said, "That's merely the ramblings of a madwoman. Let me see the letter."

"Not yet. The letter is in a safe place, and it will remain there until I get what I want."

"Well, well." He snickered. "It appears there's a cunning woman beneath that innocent façade after all. And what is it you want from me, Miss Eyre?"

"Only one thing—keep Edward from going to the gallows."

"I'm doing my best without your feeble attempt to blackmail me." He stepped out from behind the desk and moved toward me. "Even if I had been having an affair with Bertha, there's no evidence to suggest I killed her."

"No, but it moves you to the top of the suspect list."

"Not with that letter wherein Bertha instructs her survivors to look to Edward if anything happened to her."

"You wrote that letter, didn't you? Why?" I asked. "Why were you so keen on getting rid of her anyway? Were you afraid she'd have you fired after you ended the affair? That she'd report your embezzlements from Thornfield Hall to Edward?"

His brows rose. "That must be some letter."

"It is. It paints a romantic portrait of how the two of you were going to run away together. I admit I feel guilty because I had no idea what an intelligent person Bertha Rochester was when she was lucid."

Briggs moved closer to me and took me by the shoulders. "I demand to see that letter immediately. I know you're lying about its contents, you little shrew."

Reader, having a murderer put his hands on me nearly made me throw up, but I powered through.

"Bertha was in love with you, and she thought you loved her too," I said. "But you were merely taking advantage of her, weren't you? Did she threaten to tell Edward about your schemes and betrayals when she learned you were only using her? Is that why you killed her?"

Giving me a hard shake, he asked, "Why are you baiting me, Miss Eyre? If you believe me to be a murderer, then why are you so eager to make an enemy of me?"

"I'm not. I'd prefer you to be an ally."

He relaxed his hands slightly so that they were no longer biting into my upper arms, but he still didn't let me go. "Explain yourself."

"You did me a favor by ridding Edward and me of his wife. Do us another kindness in keeping Edward safe, and you won't have to embezzle—simply ask for what you need. We'll all be happy."

"You make a good argument, but someone has to pay for Bertha's murder. Any suggestions?"

"Yes, as a matter of fact, I do have our scapegoat." I lifted my chin. "St. John Rivers. He was here the night Bertha was killed, and he was here today when Grace was strangled. He can easily take the blame for both of your misdeeds."

"*Misdeeds?*" He gave a harsh laugh and dropped his hands from my arms at last. "There's ice water in your veins."

"I imagine we have that in common."

"And how to you plan to throw suspicion onto your fiancé?" he asked.

"Easy. He told me himself he visited Bertha in her bedchamber on several occasions. His sisters also know of his visits—it was Mary who told me about them. As for Grace, I could simply tell the court that she told me the night before she died that she was afraid Mrs. Rochester's killer was coming for her next. Only I'd say she was scared of St. John instead of you."

Grace hadn't told me anything, Reader. I believe adrenaline was making me bold—probably too *bold.*

"It appears you've thought of everything."

"Do we have a deal then?" I asked.

"How do I know I can trust you? Will you give me the letter now?"

"Not until after St. John's trial. Then it's yours."

Shaking his head, he said, "I hope Edward knows what he's getting himself into."

"I do." Edward opened the door to the study to reveal that he, Diana, and Blanche had been standing there listening to our entire conversation.

Briggs blustered for a second before saying, "Edward, I'm glad you're here. Otherwise, you might never have believed the treachery Miss Eyre has suggested."

"I have the letter, *Robert*," Edward said. "I've sent for the constables."

"Jane, that was ever so brave of you," Diana said.

Now that the crisis was averted, my legs threatened to turn to mush. "Thanks. I'm sorry I had to pretend to throw your brother under the b—carriage. Or, you know, to the wolves or whatever."

"It's all right. I know you and Mr. Rochester had to come up with a reasonable alternative, although everyone knows St. John wouldn't hurt a fly."

"Um…ladies."

Turning to see what Blanche had to say, I saw Briggs pointing a gun at Edward's chest. My legs did nearly give out at that point, and Diana had to help me remain standing.

"You all think you're so smart," Briggs said. "But you aren't. I could kill all of you and escape long before the constables get here."

"I refuse to let that happen." Richard stepped into the study with a rifle aimed at Briggs' head. "You will pay dearly for the murder of my sister."

I hadn't realized Richard was a part of the plan. Now here he was in a standoff with Briggs.

"Let me leave, or I'll shoot one of the women," Briggs said. He scowled at me. "*You.*" He directed his gun toward me.

"I don't care," Richard said.

Reader, I believe he meant it…which was insulting and not a little disconcerting.

"You could shoot any one of these people—even me—and I'll still manage to get off a shot," Richard continued. "I'm an excellent marksman. The only thing keeping me from killing you where you stand is Adele. I won't abandon her, much less leave her with the knowledge that I was hanged."

Briggs must have heard the truth in Richard's words because he lowered his gun. "I-I've been set up. I didn't hurt your sister. I loved her. M-Miss Eyre was right about one th-thing—B-Bertha and I were going to—"

"Stop lying!" Richard shouted. "I know about the baby!"

Burying his face in his hands, Briggs sank to his knees. "I'm sorry. Please don't kill me."

"You want me to show you mercy the way you did to my sister?" Richard snorted. "She told our sister that *R* didn't want their child, that he was afraid her madness was hereditary. Until today, I'd thought she meant Rochester. Now I know the truth."

"You're wrong," Briggs said. "I did want our baby. I—" He hushed when Richard cocked the gun.

"No more talking." Richard spoke with lethal calmness. "If you say another word, I'm going to put a bullet in your brain despite my best efforts not to do so."

Knowing he was beaten, Briggs folded into a heap and wept until the constables arrived.

But our story wasn't over yet, Reader.

CHAPTER 22

I expected Edward and me to be whisked away by Cooper as soon as the constables left Thornfield Hall with Briggs. That didn't happen.

Being a newbie to the whole book-saving thing, I decided we might have to remain until after Briggs' trial—maybe even his execution—to ensure that *Jane Eyre* and Literatia were truly safe. After all, Edward had been convicted, and here he was a free man.

At the moment, Richard was quietly apologizing to Edward for misjudging him. He'd found the letters in Edward's room and read them after we had put our plan to get Briggs to confess in motion.

"I'd come to confront you once and for all about how you'd treated my sister, not to mention your own unborn child," Richard said. "After reading the letters, I realized I'd been blaming the wrong man. I hope you can forgive me."

Edward clapped him on the shoulder. "Given the way you stepped in and kept any of us from getting shot, I absolutely forgive you."

Adele slipped her hand into mine and pulled me away from the rest of the group just as St. John was meandering in my direction. I was glad for Adele's diversion. I had no idea what St. John would say to me and even less of a clue as to what I'd say to him.

"Have you heard the news?" Adele asked. "Uncle Dickie really and truly is my uncle."

I hugged her. "That's wonderful, darling. I'm happy for you both."

"Yes, and I'm going to live with him. You'll come with us, of course, because you're my governess."

"Um…we'll get all that sorted out," I said.

Over the top of Adele's head, my eyes met Diana's. I must've been wearing a concerned expression because she gave me a slight smile and then made an announcement.

"We need to celebrate. Jane, let's go into the kitchen and ask the staff to prepare a special lunch." She laughed. "After all, it would be impolite for me to order Thornfield Hall staff around, wouldn't it?"

I didn't think I had any more authority than Diana to order anyone around, but I was all for escaping from Adele and St. John for a few minutes. And I was hungry. Lunch sounded fantastic.

Edward pinned me with a stare as I stepped around him. "Careful." He'd muttered the word under his breath.

Had he even been talking to me? It was possible he'd been speaking to Richard, telling him to be considerate of Adele.

But he'd been looking at me when he'd said the word. What did I need to be careful of? Of overstepping my boundaries at Thornfield Hall? Who cared? The killer had been caught, and the book would be resetting soon. He and I would be in North Carolina by the end of the day regaling Cooper Wellingham with tales of our adventures.

Before I could turn back and ask Edward for clarification, Diana took my arm and led me from the room. Hopefully, it wasn't Diana he'd been warning me about. She was definitely not a silverfish—unless some had better disguises than others. And Diana had been a willing participant in our plot to nab Briggs.

Surely if he'd felt I was in immediate danger, Edward would have somehow prevented me from leaving the salon.

When Diana and I stepped into the kitchen, Mrs. Fairfax was there, flanked by two other silverfish—I could tell because all three were smiling. That was unnerving.

"Good show," Mrs. Fairfax said. "You solved the mystery."

"Indeed," Diana said. "Don't you agree a celebration is in order?"

"Absolutely. To the victor go the spoils. In fact, we're already working on a splendid lunch, and it's almost ready." She nodded to her staff, and they scurried back to the counters. "Gather everyone in the dining room, and we'll be right in."

This was what Edward had been warning me about. Mrs. Fairfax was up to something. We had to watch out for her.

Diana left the kitchen, but I remained, my gaze locked on that of Mrs. Fairfax.

"Oh, go on, poppet," she said. "You've won. No need for us to try and thwart your plans now."

"But what does our winning mean to you?" I asked. "What will you do now?"

She shrugged. "I'll have a black mark on my record for sure, and I'll have to work extra hard to redeem myself."

"Is the food poisoned?"

She cackled. "Killing an entire cast of characters is against the rules. You may eat in peace."

Feeling her eyes on me as I walked out of the kitchen, I reflected on what she'd told me. The food wasn't poisoned because the silverfish weren't allowed to eliminate an entire cast of characters. Yet, if they had succeeded in destroying the book, all the characters would have been completely erased, right?

I didn't understand Mrs. Fairfax's logic. I'd ask Edward about it as soon as possible. But, for now, I was hungry. If everyone else ate, I would too.

Reader, we ate, and the food was delicious.

After lunch, tea was served. While I was sipping mine,

I noticed Mrs. Fairfax watching me from a corner of the room. Something about her smug expression sent warning bells off in my mind.

I placed my cup back on the saucer and pushed it away.

She'd said the food wasn't poisoned—she'd said nothing about the beverages. Plus, there was no need to kill every character in the book. There could be no *Jane Eyre* without Jane Eyre.

I rose from the table and glared at her. "What did you give me?"

"Whatever do you mean?" she asked.

Racing from the room, I could hear both Edward and St. John calling after me as I took the stairs two at a time. Knowing I didn't have time to waste, I ignored them and hurried to my room to get my reticule. I fumbled in the small purse and took out my tooth powder. One of the ingredients was charcoal. It wasn't necessarily *activated* charcoal—used to neutralize poisons—but it might be the only chance I had.

I poured as much of the powder into my mouth as I could at once, fighting my gag reflex as I swallowed.

"Gia!"

I turned to see Edward standing in the doorway. "She's poisoned me," I said.

St. John came to stand beside Edward. "Silly girl, what are you doing? You have that black tooth powder all over your face."

"Leave us!" Edward's voice rattled the windows of my

room.

"I—" St. John's words were drowned out as Edward pushed him out of the room and closed the door in his face.

Edward's eyes were glistening as he gathered me into his arms. "I'm sorry."

"It's not your fault. Hopefully, this nasty tooth powder will save me."

"I won't take that chance."

"You mean we can go?" I asked.

He didn't answer. He simply pressed his lips to my forehead.

I MUST'VE CLOSED my eyes because when I opened them, I was in a hospital room—a modern hospital room.

Cooper Wellingham was at my bedside. "Welcome back."

"Back...back home? I'm not in Literatia?"

"No." He smiled, but it seemed to me he was sad.

"Is everything okay? Was *Jane Eyre* restored?"

"Yes. Thank you and congratulations." He nodded toward a small suitcase at the foot of the bed. "We're free to go as soon as you get dressed and sign some papers."

I looked around the room. "Where's Edward? How long have I been in the hospital? What did Fairfax use to poison me? Where's Edward?" I know I repeated myself, but I wanted to know—*where was Edward?*

"All your questions will be answered as soon as we return to the library." He left the room.

I got out of bed and opened the case to find the clothes I'd been wearing my first day on the job. There were also all the toiletries I'd need, including my favorite brand name toothpaste. You don't realize how much you appreciate the little things until you have had to be without them.

After dressing and making myself a bit more presentable, I went to the nurses' station to sign the release papers. I didn't see Edward out in the hall. Was he waiting for us back at the manor?

The thought crossed my mind that Edward might be completely different in this world. He might be older than I'd thought or not as attractive as I'd found him in Literatia or he might be in a relationship. I gulped. He might even be married.

I tried to put all those thoughts out of my head as I rode the elevator down to the parking garage with Cooper.

Reader, if you thought Edward was standing in the parking garage with a bouquet of flowers and a welcoming kiss for me, you'd be as disappointed as I was to learn that he wasn't.

Cooper led me over to a black limo where his driver had been waiting. The chauffer opened the door for me.

No, Reader, Edward wasn't in there either.

Despite my best efforts to get him to talk, Cooper refused to discuss anything that was plaguing me until we returned to the library.

CHAPTER 23

The Smithmore Manor library had everything a booklover could possibly want. In the center of the room, two chocolate brown leather sofas sat on opposite sides of a Persian rug of muted blues, pinks, greens, and yellows. Mahogany shelves lined the walls, and two intimate reading or conversation areas—each made up of a pair of club chairs, a small round table, and a floor lamp—were positioned by the room's floor-to-ceiling windows.

The only thing missing was Edward.

"Please tell me where Edward is," I said to Cooper as soon as we'd sat on the sofa facing the door. "I don't care if he's with his family or whatever. I just want to know he's okay."

"Actually, *I'm* his family. The man you know as Edward is actually Matthew Wellingham."

Reader, the wheels in my head were spinning faster than a

sugared-up three-year-old.

"He's your son?" *Why hadn't he told me that?*

"No, dear. I'm *his* son."

After sitting there with my mouth hanging open for a moment, I said, "I don't think I heard you correctly."

"You did." Cooper stood and began to pace. "My mother's family were Gutenbergs."

"The printing press Gutenbergs?"

"The very same." He smiled briefly. "The Knights Templar gave us the responsibility of keeping valuable manuscripts safe soon after the printing press was created."

"Wait—that was in 1440. Weren't the Knights Templar dissolved in 1312?"

Give it up for me knowing my history, Reader. No way was this guy going to pull anything over on me.

Cooper inclined his head. "That's the official story. In truth, they merely went underground. Someone from the Gutenberg family line has been overseeing Literatia for hundreds of years. I took the reins from my mother forty years ago when I turned twenty-one."

I squinted at him. Math wasn't my strong suit; but if Cooper was sixty-one, that meant Edward—or, rather Matthew—had to be in his mid-seventies at the very least. "The man I met in Literatia wasn't old enough to be your father."

"That's because Dad has been trapped in Literatia for decades." He came and sat beside me. "Let me explain. There are 1440 minutes in a day, but time there is two percent of what it is here. For every day you were in Literatia, you were away from here for less than half an hour."

Raising my fingertips to my temples, I asked, "I haven't even been gone from here a day?"

"You haven't. And that's how my age has surpassed that of my own father."

"That 1440 connection between the invention of the printing press and the number of minutes in a day," I said. "Coincidence?"

He merely smiled and shrugged. "Are there truly any coincidences, Gia?"

I blew out a breath. "Okay, tell me this—when I found myself in the land of *Jane Eyre*, how was it that I was dressed appropriately? How did I have a reticule with coins and your note with me? I was here one instant wearing what I have on now, and then I was there with everyone seeing me as Jane herself. How is that possible?"

"A little bit of magic and a lot of ignorance. The people of Literatia are, for the most part, blind to the truth. Theirs is a world of fiction, so they see what they want to see. When you were part of that world, you were also corrupted to an extent by the narrative. Only Matthew and Vidocq knew you weren't Jane."

"And the silverfish—they knew."

"Yes," he said. "They know the truth but refuse to walk in it. Their goal is to destroy anything valuable, and they hate to lose. Thanks to you, they lost this battle."

"It wasn't just me." I looked around at the beautiful room. My whole experience with Literatia still seemed like a dream. "You were able to get *me* out, why not Matthew?"

"The Council of the Silverfish were intent on destroying me because I was a prodigy. That's why my mother retired early to hand the job of curator over to me. When I was a child, I could enter Literatia on my own and set worlds right."

"Where is your mom now?" I asked.

"She died twenty years ago."

"I'm so sorry. Does Matthew know?"

"He knows." He cleared his throat. "Anyway, my parents were terrified the silverfish would realize how much power I held and…well, stop me."

"Kill you, you mean."

"Eventually, they *did* realize how strong I was—"

"And that's why you can't go back there. I'm sorry, I didn't mean to interrupt, but that explains why Literatia isn't safe for you."

"Precisely. There has been a bounty on my head since I was made curator." He sighed. "That's why Dad— Matthew—allowed himself to be imprisoned by the Council. Having him there assures them that I won't completely destroy them."

"But there must be a way to get him out of there without your being hurt," I said. "We have to try."

"I've been trying. For the past thirty-five years, I've been trying."

I took his hand. "I'm here now. We'll come up with a solution together. I know we will."

"From your lips to God's ear, my dear."

There was a tap on the door before an elegant woman in a suit poked her head into the room. "Mr. Wellingham, you're needed on a call to the United Kingdom. There's a Dickens in peril."

"Excuse me, Gia. I'll be back as quickly as possible, and we'll discuss this further."

Cooper left the library, and I got up and wandered over to the shelf where I'd discovered *Jane Eyre*. The book was still there. I picked it up. The medieval *L* that had once glowed there was gone, so I didn't have the option of touching it and tumbling into the book.

I ran my hand lovingly over the cover before opening the book. There between the cover and the title page was a daisy. It was a fresh daisy. One petal had been plucked and was lying beside the flower.

She loves me was written beside it.

This was the daisy I'd playfully thrown at Edward—Matthew—during our walk. He'd picked it up and had somehow put it here for me.

A tear splashed onto the title page, and I closed the book and hugged it to me.

"I'll find you, Matthew Wellingham. I'll find you."

Go to the next page for a look at A Tale of Two Enemies, book two in the Literatia series!

A TALE OF TWO ENEMIES

G. LEESON

I was having lunch with my friend—the only person from college with whom I'd stayed in touch—and I was beginning to regret it. Don't get me wrong. I liked Connie. She was great. Plus, I had been incommunicado from everyone while I'd been taking care of my mother, so I owed it to her, and maybe to myself, to spend some time catching up.

"So, what is it you do, Gia?" Connie gazed at me as she sipped her iced tea.

But how could I possibly explain to her what I do? We were different people now. We moved in entirely different worlds. In fact, I moved between two.

Well, you see, Connie, I travel through a portal into a place called Literatia. In Literatia, there are silverfish trying to devour classic literature because why would they not? I mean, some of those books are delicious, right? Anyway, they mess up the books, and I have to go in there, find this sweetie pie named

Matthew who's kinda trapped there and has been for decades, and together we put things right so that the book is saved. Why is it so important to save the books? Well, if they're destroyed in Literatia, they disappear from our world as if they'd never existed.

Obviously, I didn't say any of that because Connie either would've recommended a good therapist or fainted on the spot. I was guessing therapist. Instead, I said, "I'm an archivist at a manor home."

Connie wrinkled her nose as she sat her glass down. "Sounds boring...and dusty."

Chuckling, I said, "The house is anything but dusty, and I'm seldom bored."

"Really? Before leaving the office to come here, I was finalizing the paperwork for a hostile takeover worth twenty million dollars." Did I mention Connie was a corporate lawyer? And, come to think of it, she sounded as if she was becoming something of a snob. "What were *you* doing?"

I supposed the truth couldn't hurt in this case. "I was reading about the French Revolution."

"Ugh. All those people getting their heads chopped off? That sounds horrible."

"Not to me. I find it fascinating." Especially since I was likely getting ready to dive headfirst into *A Tale of Two Cities*. I used my fork to pick around in my salad. I'd already eaten all the best parts of it, but I figured there might still be a bacon bit or a crouton to uncover.

There had recently been some rumblings that there

had been more *worst of times* than *best of times* within *A Tale of Two Cities*. Granted, the book totally dwells on those *worst of times* since it's all about Madame Defarge wanting Charles Darnay and his entire family sent to the guillotine because his father and uncle were responsible for the death of her sister. But this was different. This was silverfish-induced *worst of times*.

Connie shrugged. "I'm glad you like it." Her tone implied she'd rather have bamboo shards shoved under her fingernails. "Are you seeing anyone?"

"No." The man I was seeing—or, rather, wanted to see—was in Literatia, so a simple *no* would have to suffice. "You?"

"There's an attorney in our office who has asked me out a couple of times. He's cute, but if it didn't work out, I'd be stuck seeing him all the time unless one of us transferred. And I'm definitely not leaving. My career is really taking off."

"Still, I suppose you could go on one date and see if you have anything in common," I said.

"I don't know. I might." She took another drink. "Is there anyone you could set me up with? What about your boss? Is he handsome?"

"He is, but I don't think he's in the market for a girl-friend right now. Besides, he's old enough to be our dad." Hypocritical aside here, the guy I was crushing on was even older, but it was different. Time moved much slower in Literatia, so he wasn't—biologically speaking—all that old.

"Who cares? Is he rich?" she asked.

Reader, was there a nice way to say none of your business? If there was, it eluded me at that moment.

"Are you joking, or have you always been this shallow?" The words slipped out before I'd realized it. They hung there between us like an awkward, heavy chain stretching from my mouth to her ear. No way to reel them back in, so I forced out a laugh.

She laughed too. "You had me going there for a second!"

"You're so easy to tease!" My phone rang, and I said a silent prayer of thanksgiving. "I need to take this." I slid my chair back, stood, and walked out into the lobby of the restaurant. "Josephine, is everything okay?"

"I realize you're—" She sighed. "We need you back. As quickly as possible."

"I'm on my way." I returned to the table to tell Connie I had to go. "I'll pay the check on my way out."

"I won't hear of it. Lunch is on me." She made a shooing motion with both hands. "You hurry back to your French Revolution. I'm going to linger here for a few minutes more."

"All right." I bent and gave her a one-armed hug. "Thanks!" I hurried out of restaurant. As eager as I was to see what was wrong at Smithmore Manor, I was even more keen on escaping this uncomfortable lunch.

I HURRIED into the library where Josephine, wearing white cotton gloves, was sitting on the sofa with the gilt-embossed copy of Charles Dickens' first edition *A Tale of Two Cities.* I'd been poring over the book a couple of days ago when there were only minor glitches in the story.

"What's happened?" I looked around the room. "Where's Cooper?"

"He went upstairs to lie down. He's not feeling well."

I sat beside her on the sofa. "Is it that bad?" Opening my purse, I took out my own white cotton gloves and slipped them on so I could handle the book. I couldn't imagine anything worse than *Jane Eyre's* hero, Edward Rochester, being found guilty of his wife's murder; but that hadn't made Cooper take to his bed. That had only made him shove me into the deep end of the pool, so to speak, where I'd had to sink or swim.

"Dr. Manette has been murdered." With a sigh, Josephine closed the book and handed it to me.

"How—? When?" My questions were tumbling over each other in my head.

"I found it right before I called you. You're going to have to go into the book at once."

Sitting there cradling the book on my lap, I felt like an idiot. I had no idea how to travel to Literatia without Cooper. Heck, I didn't know how to go into the book *with* Cooper. I swallowed the lump in my throat. "Do you know how to get me there?"

She nodded. "I'm nowhere near as accomplished as Cooper, but I put you where you need to be. You'll be going in as Lucie Manette. Matthew is already there as Charles Darnay."

"My husband." I clamped my lips together. That was twice in less than an hour that I wished I'd kept my mouth shut. "I mean, where in the book are we?"

"Yes, you're married," she said, slipping off her gloves.

"Oh, good. That will make communication so much easier."

Seriously, Reader, my feelings had very little to do with being able to walk around with my arm hooked through his or being able to steal a chaste kiss now and then. It was hard for an unmarried woman to communicate with a man unchaperoned back in the day.

Ignoring my interruption, she continued. "You've had to forego your honeymoon due to the death of Lucie's father."

"Then neither of us killed him." I brightened. "That's nice to know."

Josephine rubbed the bridge of her nose. "Are you ready to go?"

I hesitated. Preparation hadn't been an option before I was sent into *Jane Eyre*. "Is there anything you feel I should know or that I should do?"

"Only to be careful, but you know that."

"Should I read about the murder? Do you think that would help?"

"There's nothing to read. Miss Pross found the man lying face down on the floor in the parlor," she said. "That's all we've got at this point."

"I'd like to see Cooper before I go." I placed the book on the side table before I took off my gloves and returned them to my purse. "Where's his room?"

She shook her head. "No. He needs his rest, and I won't have him disturbed. Besides, you have work to do."

Cooper had seemed fine this morning. And he was still relatively young. I'd never known him to go to bed sick. Granted, I'd only been here a few days.

"Does he have some sort of condition I'm not aware of?" I asked.

"He'll be fine. You need to go. Now."

"What do I need to do?" When I'd been transported into *Jane Eyre* by Cooper, I reached for a book, placed my hand on a glowing *L*, and found myself on a street in Victorian England not having a clue as to what was going on.

Josephine nodded toward the book lying on the table. A glowing *L* was now on the cover.

"Just put my hand on it?" I asked.

"Yes. Fingers crossed it's going to work."

Reader, it didn't work. Rather than getting ready to board a ship with my new husband, I found myself standing at the back of a small church wearing a rose-colored dress with a pouf skirt preparing to walk down the aisle on the arm of Dr. Manette!

ACKNOWLEDGMENTS

I'd like to thank Shannon, Michelle, Eleanor, Larry, Benjamin, Jessica, and, of course, Zoltan who helped inspire An Eyre of Mystery at the Smithmore Castle Writers Retreat in 2021. Thanks, too, to fellow writers Jennifer, Melissa, and Erin for being sounding boards and to my wonderful family for believing in me even when I'm ready to give up writing altogether and go to work for Spirit Halloween (which I think would be really fun if I could just get paid for dressing up and playing with Halloween props). Last, but certainly not least, if you're looking for some amazing cover art, check out covervillain.com.

ABOUT THE AUTHOR

G. Leeson might appear to be new to writing, but she's better known as Gayle Leeson. As Gayle Leeson, she writes cozy mysteries; but a marketing expert warned her that cozy readers might not follow her into the portal fantasy realm. She, on the other hand, will read just about anything. If you'd like to see what else Gayle has written, please visit her website at https://www.gayleleeson.com/.

If you'd like to get an exclusive prequel to the series and learn how Cooper was introduced to Literatia, click here to read Saving Piglet.